DES DILLON was born and brought up in Coatbridge, Lanarkshire, in 1960, and read English at Strathclyde University. A former teacher, he is now a poet, short story writer, novelist and dramatist writing for radio, stage, television and film, and has been a scriptwriter for *High Road* and *River City*. He has taught Creative Writing at the Arvon Foundation, and was Writer in Residence at Castlemilk, Glasgow, between 1998 and 2000. Des now lives in Galloway.

To date he is the author of seven novels and one poetry collection. His novel, *Me and Ma Gal*, was shortlisted for the Saltire Society Scottish First Book of the Year Award and won the 2003 World Book Day 'We Are What We Read' poll for the novel that best describes Scotland today. It is to be broadcast as a drama on Radio 4 in 2004. A short film of *Duck* was premiered at Edinburgh Film Festival in 1998 and in 2003 his play *Lockerbie 103* went on national tour. Des orginally wrote *Six Black Candles* as a play which won the International Festival of Playwriting Award in 2001, and in 2004 played at the Royal Lyceum Theatre in Edinburgh.

I think it's a modern Scottish classic... I've read it three times. It's romantic, true, honest and very sensitively done, so sparely written that each word counts. There's an assumption out there that Des Dillon is a yobbo from the sticks. In reality, he's anything but – and he's a cunning, sophisticated writer.
GILES GORDON, THE SCOTSMAN

This first novel is a Scottish Classic – no, a classic which is Scottish. Read it.
KATE BLACKADDER, SCOTTISH BOOK COLLECTOR

This is a well nigh perfect balancing act.
DOUGLAS GIFFORD, BOOKS IN SCOTLAND

Also by Des Dillon:

Fiction
The Big Empty: A Collection of Short Stories (1996)
Duck (1998)
Itchycooblue (1999)
Return of the Busby Babes (2000)
The Big Q (2001)
Six Black Candles (2002)
The Glasgow Dragon (2004)

Poetry
Picking Brambles (2003)

Me and Ma Gal

DES DILLON

Luath Press Limited

EDINBURGH

www.luath.co.uk

First published in 1995 by Argyll Publishing
First Headline Review edition 2001
First Luath edition 2004

Des Dillon has asserted his rights under the Copyright, Designs and
Patents Act 1988 to be identified as the author of this work.

The paper used in this book is recyclable.
It is made from low-chlorine pulps produced in a low-energy,
low-emission manner from renewable forests.

Printed and bound by
Bookmarque Ltd., Croydon

Typeset in 9.5 point Frutiger
by Jennie Renton

For the bold Gal.
You shared the most
dazzling days of my life.

Picking brambles;
sunshine wilting
on late September shoulders.
Remember the burns and rivers
rubbing water on the browning backs
of me and Stevie Gallacher.

The rain falls
like a curtain call.
Sun ships between clouds
and rainbow roars its encore
to a world that is forever moving on
and leaving Stevie Gallacher
splashing in moving memory.
And me?
I'm picking brambles all the while.

Me and Ma Gal

Me and Ma Gal

I mind the first time I ever seen the bold Gal. Well, I might have seen him before cos you can never tell. I mean I might have walked by him in the street but I never even knew what he looked like so I don't really know if I ever saw him. But I guess that I must've. Where we lived was the kind of place that you could see someone you never knew... and the next day you'd know them.

Anyway, I met him this day. He was kickin a stone about at the bottom of the lane of houses we had just flitted into. We called it The Lane cos it was a lane but it was ours. It was as wide as me an Gal bein two planes, touchin wing tips an there was a row of five-apartment houses on each side... full of hundreds of wanes. You could be a plane an land in it. Sometimes I'd have propellers that hardly worked, an even with one wing fallin off, I could land in the lane safe. It was even safer with Gal commandin me in from up there in one of the lamp posts. The lane was that long they gave us two lamp posts.

Sometimes it was a rushy football pitch. I never was very good at the rushy football but you couldn't beat me at Time Racin round the block. Gal always brought people to race me an every time I used to tank them, so I did. God, you should've seen me zoomin about – like Billy Whizz – down the lane, leanin into The Houses as I churned round the corner. Sometimes ma face was so close to the roughcast that people, Gal an them, would think *he's goin to scrape his face off that wall an then he'll need to go to hospital*... they never ever said that but that was what they used to think; every time I sped into a corner they thought it. It was one of them things that you just know.

The only time I nearly got beat is when I whizzed round a corner an cracked heads with Jerry Brolly. I seen birds an stars like in the Beano but I ran on, jammin ma left eye open with ma fingers. Jerry was fat an slow so I went slow so that I could stagger over the finishin line just in time (Linda Curie an Ellen Rettie always watched the Time Racin), with the cut I had from us crashin into each other.

Well!

I nearly never got there on time cos Jerry Brolly came blubberin down the lane early an I had to break out of the wounded stagger and put a spurt on or he'd've won.

Anyway, The Lane was our bit, once you got there, no matter what you were runnin from, you were home.

So. I'm at the bottom of this here lane that I'm bumpin ma gums about. I'm down there like a dog markin out new territory. All the time I kept a right good lookout for any **Big Guys** cos they were always on the lookout for some of us so that they could terrorise us with them hatchets that's made out of a bean tin bashed down, flat, over a stick. I knew all about that from the oul house.

Next thing I knows is a guy comes kickin a stone past me.

Past me again.

Past me again.

I knew he wanted to talk to me but was too scared to talk. He looked as if he knew that I wanted to talk to him but that I was too scared too.

I looked tough.

He kicked the stone an looked tough back at me. I was just about to spit an show him who was boss when he brought one up from halfway down his gullet an grogged it onto the new slabs. As if that wasn't enough, while I was thinkin about somethin tough to do back to him he rolled the stone into the grogger. With his left hand in his pocket he turns round an crushes his face at me. For a minute I thinks it's like a plate of porridge but I don't laugh. In some kind of answer I dug ma heel into the ground hundreds of times. I surprised myself at ma strongness an the massive hole that I made in the ground. Gal just turned back to his stone.

I put ma two hands behind me an lifted myself onto the fence. It was diggin into the back of ma legs but I never wanted him to know that so I never screamed or said… *this is dead sore*… or anythin like that. I just looked at the Workies' Huts at the bottom of the lane as if I knew somethin about them that he didn't.

Well that done the trick cos there he was starin at the grey Workies' Compound then at ma face. I shrunk ma eyes like Awday Murfy in the cowboy films so that he'd know I was onto somethin he never knew nothin about.

He looks at the huts.

He looks at me.

I knew he was just about to speak. But you can't just ask a guy what he's thinkin cos that gives him the bossy seat, so Gal had to say somethin that would get him tough enough to go with the stone an the grog he had done for me a minute ago.

I jumps off the fence an wandered about so that he could get the time to think of somethin to say. Some buildin trucks roared by an threw clouds of desert dust at us so that we waved our hands so that we could see. You had to shut your eyes so our hands kept on slapping thegether. Gal started to choke at me so I choked back at him. I always member that as the first thing we done thegether; we choked and slapped hands. I always used to say to Gal that there can't be a lot of people who started hangin about thegether after slappin hands an nearly gettin choked to death with desert dust. It was a dangerous place, a scheme that

3

was all half-built houses and piles of rubble.

After the dust went away we could see each other an we never needed to choke any more. We just eyed each other up an down an ignored each other an followed each other about... if you know what I mean.

I was just decidin to go back up the lane into our new house with two toilets when he looks at me an I knew he was goin to talk. I never wanted to put him off so I leaned forward, goggled ma eyes an opened ma mouth so that he knew that I knew he was just about to talk. I learnt that from Teachers.

What's your name? I looks at him.

He looks at me. *Eh?*

I asked him leanin forward nearly fallin over. I could lean forward more than anybody I knew. People used to always say that about me; *he can't half lean forward him* they used to say when I wasn't there. Gal looked amazed at that too.

He spits, out the side of his top lip, in a friendly sort of way an says again: *What's your name then?*

Derruck Daniel Riley.

I looks at him waitin for him to tell me what a crackin name I had. He stopped an took it all in, you could tell he was doin that cos even though his eyes were open they weren't really lookin at anythin... they were lookin at the things inside his head. It made me feel good that he was lookin inside his head at ma name. He thought for ages about it. I thought I was goin to miss ma dinner. After ages an ages he jags his finger up in the air about the height of his ear. I knew he was goin to speak. By this time in life I was gettin quite good at tellin when people were goin to speak.

Derruck Riley?... Derruck Danyul Riley?

He was well jarred with that name. I could tell cos he shouted it out loud an laughed a tiny bit after he said that. People

4

always laughed when you shocked them with somethin good. Specially a good name.

Derruck Danyul Riley... Derruck Danyul Riley... He kept on saying that walking round in a circle like it was some kind of Wizard or Warlock spell he was doin.

This time I wasn't really sure what way he was sayin it. For a minute I thought he was laughin at me but I still felt good. It felt good cos the only people that called you Derrick Daniel Riley was the Teachers an Father Boyle. An when they said it always made you feel bad – as if you done somethin wrong – it made you shrink dead wee like when Priests talk to you.

An what's your name?

You could tell he wanted me to ask that cos he turns away an kids on that he never heard me. But I knew that he heard me cos he paused a bit when he kidded on that he was just turnin away as I asked him. I decided that I liked him an that's why I asked him again.

I said what's your name?

Oh... right... ma name... Steven... Gallacher...

Steven withaVnotaPH. He looks me right in the eye. I looks at him. Even though it sounded dead interestin, you know, all this V an PH stuff, I couldn't think of anythin to say. I wanted to say somethin about it. I know that it was somethin really important cause of the way he was actin but I still never thought of anythin to say. He was waitin.

That's good, I said lookin at him to see if that was good enough. He seemed happy with the fact that it was good an shook his head an soldiers from side to side, smilin. He always done that did the Gal fellah. He always used to bounce from side to side if he was really happy or chuffed with somethin he done. But he specially done it when someone else told him that somethin he done was really good. Sometimes he'd do that to me when he beat me at cards an it made me ragin.

After all that action we were quiet for a while. We had to think.

He got a bigger stone an kicked it around a bit. He never spat this time. I think he was happy an that's why he never spat. I jumped back onto the fence again. This time I was happy an it never mattered to me how hard the fence was diggin into me no way was I goin to scream now.

The Tecs

Well, me an Gal started hangin around thegether. The town was criss-crossed by millions an millions of railways. They went everywhere so they did. You couldn't go anywhere an you'd come to a railway. All the towns on the telly had rivers – we had railways. You always had to cross one. If you didn't go over the tracks you had to go round the long way an you'd have to be krazy or oul or really scared of trains to go round the long way. Goin round the long way always took ages an ages. Sometimes I went the long way if I was on ma own. That's how I know how long it takes. But me an Gal never took the long way.

Everywhere we went we never took the long way. Honest! We used The Railways every time we went out. But to get to the story I'm supposed to tell you. Oh! that's right you probably don't know about this story. Well our Teacher told us to magine we were tellin someone about the most membered bit when you were young. This is what was on the board:

Write a story about a day in your childhood which really left an impression on you. Imagine you are actually telling the story to someone other than your Teacher. Check spelling and punctuation before you hand this in. The best story will get a Fizzy Lizzy and two MB bars.

We're supposed to magine a person we are telling it to. So I'm telling it to you. This is ma story about the time someone was goin about killin boys that were the same age as me an Gal. Our Maws an Das were never done tellin us to stay away from The Railway an The Burn an up The Lochs. An they always used to shout,

How many times have I told you not to go

near them effin railways?!!?

An you felt like sayin ten or twelve or somethin but you never. Well, you could if you wanted a swift cuff on the ear.

That's why I'm tellin this story cause two boys had already been found dead. Strangled an abyoosed. One was dead for three weeks before they found him under The Pipe at The Burn. Gal even knew the dead boy's cousin! You couldn't get near it for all us after the Fuzz were away. We were crawling through each others legs to get there. The other one was found in bushy bits up The Lochs. He was strangled an abyoosed too. I knew it would never happen to me an Gal. We were too clever an the bold Gal knew some neat moves. But our Maws an Das acted as if you were goin to get it the next time you walked out the effin door, like we were number one on his list an Strangler Joe was waitin in the back shed specially for you! That never frightened us.

Trains frightened me an Gal sometimes, like, they'd sneak up behind you an blow that big horn.

WOOO HOOO they'd go.

Sometimes you could hear it through your feet. That made you jump so it did, it really made you jump. Nobody ever never jumped when a train sneaked up behind them an blasted its horn. I don't care what they say it's an impossibility. You've got to jump and that's that. They said that trains went on the left. They're always sayin stupid things like that: *Trains always run on the left... trains always run on the left...*

Aye! right yar, I mean how are you supposed to know what one is the right an what one is the left? That's right, you can't tell, an me an Gal used to go for miles an miles on the tracks without knowin what was left an right. So you can see that, if you never knew your railways, it could be a really dangerous place. But we had a plan for trains. We always had a plan. Even for Strangler Joe.

But the best plan was the one that we kept for The Railway Tecs. Boy were they daft. Sometimes the Train Tecs would try an get you. They must've thought that we were daft as well cos they used to shout from miles away:

STOP RIGHT THERE!!

We would always stop when they shouted that. I was great at stoppin when they shouted. I'd kind of stop dead as if I had been frozen to the spot by their magic shout. I seen it in a film. Gal'd just copy me cos he never could do it as good. We always copied each other if we weren't sure. It was spooky. If I was rubbish at somethin Gal could always do it great an the other way round, I could do great things that Gal couldn't do.

Amazin.

So there we were – stopped as anythin – an we'd always look half daft at each other. The Tecs would think, *Hello hello this is our lucky day* an run full force at us. They got bigger an bigger an we laughed more an more. Sometimes I'd get a wee bit scared cos Gal'd leave it ages before he gave the secret signal to run. Three short clicks like Skippy an

BOUNCE

we were off. They got right next to us an Gal gave the three clicks. We ran like Lintees in different directions. We always done that, ran in different directions that was our best plan. If there was somethin you knew us for it was for runnin in

9

different directions. We used to amaze people with that one so we did. We would meet at a certain place that we agreed on earlier. Every mornin when we met we would say a place. The Oil Pond, The Slaggy, The Gravy, The Widdy or somethin. We were two smart cookies all right me an the Gal fellah. We left them Tecs scratchin their heads. They never knew what to do. Sometimes I felt sorry for the Tecs. Makin them look so daft an that. There they were scratchin their heads, a right pair of twadgers, sweatin, fat an red, or skinny an grey (you only got two kinds of Tecs).

It was worse if we used to call them all the names under the sun... sometimes I never wanted to shout at them but you felt like it was your duty. It was them an us. Everybody in Coatbridge felt it was them an us. Sometimes they'd call us Fenian Bastards. The first time I asked ma Maw what that was an she said,

Get out of ma road I'm makin the dinner.

That was a better answer than usual. She usually said,
That's great son... that's great son.
Sometimes I went like this: *Maw... Maw... I just killed this guy... bashed him to death with a swish roll... chocolate.*
That's great son... that's great son.
There was eleven of us so she was always makin the dinner or somethin. I only ever seen her backside cos she was always facin away doin this an that. She'd show her face at weddins an that. But ma Da knew what it was an he told me:
It means Catholic son... Fenian means Catholic... who was it called you that?
The Train Tecs and we weren't even over the fence we were just lookin at the trains goin...
He closed the door as he left the room an I could hear the

music for the news. To this day I don't know what big people see in the news. So that's how I knew what Fenian meant. The thing that I could never understand - me an Gal wondered for a whole afternoon about it - was how they knew that me an Gal were Catholics plus... how could they tell such detail from so far away. Big Gal – Gal's Da – said it must've been the way we walked. We went outside the Chapel an watched them coming out... he was right they did walk funny.

Like I said, sometimes I'd feel sorry for the Tecs an I felt bad about callin them all the names under the sun, but I don't think Gal felt bad about it. I never asked him, it's just that his eyes used to light up when he was screaming *tell tale tit your mammy canny knit* and all that stuff. They always shouted one thing or the other:

1. *We'll get you ya wee bastards.*

2. *We'll get you ya wee Fenian bastards.*

We knew that they had to see the way that you walked to shout number two. Anyway, they must've shouted that a million times an they never caught us. We were too smart for them tubes. Funny thing was, when they shouted that you stopped feelin sorry for them. This was when I'd wonder how I ever felt sorry for them an I'd feel proud an angry at the same time. If we were in a really bad mood – like when some of the bigger boys had gave us a doin an took our stuff off us – this was when we would sneak back up on the Tecs as they scratched their head like Laurel and Hardy.

We'd lob a few half-bricks over the fence at them. Boy they hated that so they did. They really hated that. They'd run faster than their bodies could take an be too puffed to climb the fence. We'd make faces at them an wiggle our bums. Sometimes we'd press our faces into the criss-cross wire and flick our tongues; they'd keep sticking their fingers through the fence trying to grab us. You could tell they really hated us. They'd tell us how they were goin to rip us to bits. Man they'd slabber an foam an we'd laugh an laugh an point at them rubbin our bellies in circles with the other hand. We learnt that from the comics. They hated that too. When they started to rustle in the ground for bricks or sticks to poke us, we

left the area pronto,

laughin like Woody the Woodpecker.

Ha Ha Ha Haaa Ha
Ha Ha Ha Haaa Ha
Ha Ha Ha Haaa Ha
Ha Ha Ha Haaa Ha

I think they hated that too.

But to tell you the truth, I liked it better when the Tecs weren't there. I'm mad so I am, most other boys like to fight but I liked it quiet most of the time. I always knew when they weren't there, don't ask me how I knew that. I just did. Gal used to ask me. We would sneak out of The Railway Trees an I'd look left an right an he'd ask, *Are they there?*

I'd pause for a couple of seconds so that the quiet would make me important an then answer.

Gal always took ma word for it. In all the times we were on the tracks I was never wrong. It was magic when I'd scrunch out of the darkness an green of the trees an know that they weren't there. They were useless anyway, I mean, the trains could sneak up on you easier than them an that horn blastin gave you more of a fright. Sometimes you'd think that the Tecs never wanted to catch no one.

The best times were in the hotness of the summer.

In the summertime da da da da da da da da da da da...

That would be Gal singin the same bit over and over an noddin his head side to side.

Sing the rest of the song Gal.

No I like this bit the best... In the Summertime when the weather is fine da da da da da da da da da da da...

I bet you don't know the rest.

He looks at me with the *oh do you bliddy think so* look.

Go on... sing it then I says.

In the Summertime when the weather is fine da da da da da da da da da da...

The rest!

He laughs and goes,

In the Summertime when the weather is fine da da da da da da da da da... You can stretch right up and tou...ouch The Sky... you got wimmin you got wimmin on your mind.

He kept goin. Had me beat there so off I pops right along the tracks there an there's Gal doin the walk an the whole bit now.

Have a drink have a drive go out an see what you can find... In the Summertime when the weather is fine da da da da da da da da da da da...

The Bricklayer

You could look along the tracks an things would appear an disappear in the heat. I used to think the tracks were breathin in the sun. Man they used to glitter. They don't glitter like that no more. It must be the trains that rub the glitter out of them after so long. An I mind the smell of the oil an the diesel, that went with the breathin tracks an the glitter an the heat. It was brill to see the tracks move but it was a million times better when you were tired an trampin slow an you could suck that oily smell right up your nose an magine you were in a film about a couple of escaped guys that walk along a railway for miles.

Ah, Bisto!

the Gal used to say. An even if I heard it hundreds of times before I used to laugh cos we were just like them Bisto kids on the adverts. Except we were two boys an they were a boy an a girl an we never ran in right away when our Maws shouted that the dinner was ready or something. *Ah Bisto!* they'd go with their funny wee clothes on an run away in like in The House was the best place in the solar system.

We were always goin somewhere else an not arrivin. We'd get stopped on the way by some adventure or some place to explore an before you knew it we'd get killed if we never went home. So we had to abort the mission. That nearly always happened.

Anyway, the day that I am thinkin of tellin you about we had left the bushes after I peeped out. There was no Tecs. We walks onto the track to our left. As I said we never found out what their left was. We only walked a wee bit along the tracks this time cos we had to get over the Mill Brae bridge that goes over the road that goes under it. This was the most dangerous bit of all cause that was where the guard (they called him **The Bricklayer**) used to always try to kill you if he seen you on the tracks. It never mattered what age or size you were, if he seen you, you were dead meat an that was that. Hundreds of people had got killed by him. But he was in his rights – Gal said that he heard his Da sayin that if a man muddered someone who broke into his house he was in his rights. So it was obvious that The Bricklayer was in his rights here to kill you. But that never kept us away from that bit. In fact, you might find this hard to believe but it made you want to go there more. In the summer holidays the place was jam-packed with gangs tryin not to get killed. Man it was a dangerous place. We got the careful walk on an we done the eyes that we always do when we are in a place we can get killed. We done the turnin round dead slow all the time an all.

Keep your eyes peeled for the krazy bastard! Gal said without-out shiftin his eyes from the part where the track swipes out of view. He never used to swear an now he was startin to do it once, sometimes twice a day. I never swore cos I'd get thundered for it. Ma Da swore. So did Gal's but he had hundreds of big brothers an they showed him how to swear. Sometimes he never came out cos he was practisin the swearin. Sometimes The Polis used to bring some of Gal's brothers home. It was funny, they were all called Gal, even the sisters. The Maw, Mary Gal, used to stick her head out the door an shout:

Gaaaaaal yer dinner's on the table, come in here right now fur yer eggs chips n beans.

After about a couple of seconds you could hear runnin feet. After another couple of seconds all these different Gals would be runnin at the gate as if the Pope of Rome was in their house. The Da would always get his dinner first so there was no use in runnin. But they always done it, they ran every time an there would be Gal the Da shufflin home from the pub. He liked to drink every day if he could manage it. It must be hard gettin to the pub with a house an wanes an all that but Da Gal done it nearly every day. The funny thing was that Mrs Gal asked him where he was every day like she never knew where he was.

An where the hell have you been all day?!!?

Even I knew the answer to that. One day I goes *He was in McKenzie's bar Mrs Gallacher.*

She looks at me as if I just killed her cat an then shouts to Gal.

Steven you come in here right this minute.

Gal'd scuffle in lookin at the pavement an then dash past her to dodge the slap on the head. She'd look at me with a face you'd see in the girls yard at school an walk in slammin the door. There was always a quiet bit here an then shoutin an bawlin an then a couple of slaps. Five minutes later you'd see Gal at the window signallin to me about what we were doin the next day or playin with the dud batteries I sold him.

No wonder he took up the swearin, you need a hobby in a house like that one.

So, as I was sayin, there we were on The Railway at the very bit where The Bricklayer used to kill people. He used to have a pile of bricks on his guards wagon an he'd launch them from the movin train at anythin that moved. He was always in SOME MOOD so he was. We never seen him but we knew every wrinkle on his face. Mick Rettie seen him five times. He used to hang from a tree wearin green things an look right at The

Bricklayer's face. We used to pay Mick money an stuff to tell us what The Bricklayer looked like. We were fly like that me an the Gal cos we knew what he looked like an if we ever saw him we would use our Different Directions plan an that would stump him. So, thanks to Mick we were always on the lookout for a big fat red face with a pirate patch, shaved head, the end of his nose bit off an only one ear. That description was well worth the money. You'd think two guys as clever as me an Gal were as well stayin well out his road – the amount of people he had killed with his bricks. But it was funny, there we were stood right there waitin on him.

Gal said that they called him The Bricklayer as a kind of joke.

A JOKE?

I never could see to this day how that was funny. I mean, Snottery Beak, or Fat Face, they're jokes. HIS name used to frighten me no end. Still does. Not that we were easy to frighten, me an Gal, no way, me an Gal thegether we could face anythin, we were like boys in a film, but The Bricklayer, well he scared me. I never wanted to die.

I didn't know if Gal never wanted to die, I never asked him. Anyway, Gal said that his big cousin, Doc, who lived near The Valley – that was the name of the place where the train ran through, it was a steep sided valley runnin down to a burn an a stinkin sewer – his cousin told him that The Bricklayer used to have nothin up with him till one night in summer he took his wife an wane out on the guards wagon for a hurl. That very night a gang of boys from down The Valley way threw a con-crete block off a bridge. The block went crashin down through the trees an through the roof of the guards wagon. It killed the wife an the wane. After that The Bricklayer declared war on anyone that dared to go down The Valley when his train was goin by.

Even after Gal told me the truth of the matter I still wondered why anyone would want to kill me an Gal. We never done nothin to nobody that would make them want to kill us. It sent shakers all over me to think of anyone killin me. At least with The Bricklayer it would be quick an you'd have a kind of idea why he done it. But Strangler Joe? Now he WAS scary. I looks around for him. With The Bricklayer I sometimes thought that if I smiled at him kind enough, as if I liked him an that, he'd mibbi let us off with just a head bashin or somethin. I never took the chance cos I was too scared even to look at the wagon never mind The Bricklayer.

Shh.

Gal stopped with his arms stretched out an his head tilted down to the front. That was when he was in a good listenin position when he stood like that. He had a right good pair of ears on him did Gal, a right good pair. They even stuck out a bit so that he could hear. Some people used to call him the Wing Nut an stuff like that but I always wanted ears that stuck out for hearin better.

I stopped an waited for him to listen. I never moved a muscle an I could hear The Burn runnin by at the bottom of The Valley. I could hear the big fans in the sewer spinnin round an round. Sometimes it would make me sick to think about the big fans in the sewer. Not the smell just the turnin fans an the noise.

It was no good askin him anythin when he was listenin cos he'd just look up an widen his eyes at you so that you'd know to shut up so that he could listen. I waited. I even opened ma mouth dead wide so that the noise of the air draggin on ma lips wouldn't annoy Gal.

Hold on he says, with his arms to the side like he was stoppin a whole army of men. He sinks onto his hunkers an spits on the track an rubs it in. He always done that in the summer. He spat on the track to cool it down. Sometimes if the sun was too hot your ear could get stuck to the track if you never spat on it first. Gal was an expert. He always spat on it first in the summer. He rubbed it in with one finger. In the winter he'd rub it hard too cos on a cold day you could get welded to the track with Jack Frost. It must be scary bein welded to the track an a train comin. Me an Gal used to argue about what would be the worst: welded to the track facin the train or welded to the track so that you never seen the train comin. We never got an answer but I think you'd be better lookin away from the train.

I bet The Tecs wouldn't save you then. No way. Gal got into position an pressed his ear on the line. He held onto it too, with both hands like he was feelin it for vibrations an that. He was always quiet when he done that but this time you knew that there was a train comin cos when there was a train comin the quiet was always a different quiet from the quiet that you heard when there was no train comin. Sometimes it used to member me of the horror films when the monster was about to come in the window or through the wall or somethin. Gal swivelled his eyes up.

It's at least a Thirty-Sixer, could be bigger.

Christ!

I said, cause a Thirty-Sixer was somethin. I had only ever seen a Twenty-Niner an even Gal only ever seen a Thirtyer.

He listened some more. I knew he was makin sure. He never made a mistake before but this was special. This was at least a Thirty-Sixer an he had to make double sure that he was right. Ma eyes were riveted on the bit where the tracks disappeared round the bend. I don't know how I never thought of it then...

I mean... no matter what length the train was the front of it was always goin to be the same. But there I was, like a right tube lookin at this bend in the line an waitin for a train that would be at least a hundred feet high. I was gettin more an more terrified by the minute.

Gal's still listenin an all I can hear is the birds whistlin in the trees an The Burn burblin far below. Somehow this scared me too. I kept maginin the noise of a big train crashin into the noise of the wee birds an the water, I can't really explain it but I know what I mean. I was scared of a noise cause it was goin to waste a noise that I liked. Gal came back into the noise.

Yup... I was right... definitely a Thirty-Sixer but it could be as big as a Fortyer.

Jesus!

I said that half cause I was amazed an half cause I wanted him to feel good about findin out the size of the train. This could be our first ever Fortyer, we should have been happy but we were really afraid. Gal jumps up dustin down the fronts of his trousers, which are the only clean bit of them anyway. He repeats what he said:

Yup, it's a Fortyer all right.

He nodded his head as he spoke. Gal used to always talk like a cowboy when he was doin things like listenin for trains or smellin the air to see if it was goin to rain or followin some animal tracks. I used to think that he should really be talkin like an Indian at them times but I never said, I wanted him to feel good.

You know something? he asks puttin both fists on his hips to make it important.

What?

I knew that this was somethin important for two reasons.

One, like I already said, Gal had his two fists on his hips an the way that he spoke. He moved a bit closer to me as if it was a secret he was tellin me.

Our Pluff told me that The Bricklayer only ever went on trains that are bigger than a Thirty-Fiver. Well that means that this train could be The Bricklayer.

Ma heart jumped but I don't think Gal seen it. I leaned a little forwards an sort of bulged ma eyes so that he'd need to come up with an answer to our problem.

This is nearly a Fortyer. Best thing we can do is hide in the trees or somethin like that so if it is The Bricklayer we might get a look at him.

I shook with fear for a couple of seconds.

Are you OK?... you look a bit white.

Aye... I just tripped over that stone there. I hits the stone a kick an follows Gal but ma eyes are fixed on the bend in the tracks.

Let's get into position then.

As he said that you could hear the slight sound of the train comin up the track. Ma heart beat faster an faster. It was like the train was warnin that it was comin. You couldn't see it yet but you knew that it was there. By this time we were through the fence an hidin in the grass. A bright yellow train front appeared on the bend an for a moment the noise stopped. It was weird. The train came round on its left but that was our right as we looked at it... that really mixes you up. I don't know where they get their ideas from, so I don't.

By this time Gal had dived deep into the grass an all you could see was his brown hair. But he was a clever customer was the Gal. It was like he was readin ma thoughts cos just as I was thinkin that I could see his brown hair stickin up out of the grass he reaches out an grabs a clump of grass an sticks it on his head.

After some thought he reaches up to a tree that's hangin down from The Sky almost to the ground an breaks off a load of twigs. He sticks that in his hair along with the stuff already in it. My God he looked magic. Camelfladge was his game all right. He looked like a strange bush growin above the waves of green grass on the slope.

I got down beside him an done the same. There we were like two bushes. Perfect. We felt like two sojers on a special mission. I never asked Gal if he felt like that I just knew that he did. There's somethin about not gettin seen when you can see all the things that are goin on all around you. It made you feel sort of powerful, it was a good feelin, as if you don't exist. Then we thought that we were two rabbits lyin in the grass scared of that guy with the gun, Elmer Fudge, or somethin.

The noise of the train got louder an we could just see it yellow in the distance through the grass.

It's a long yin all right, said Gal. *This must be The Bricklayer's train right enough.*

The noise got louder an louder. It was gettin so loud that I wanted to run but I couldn't. I looked at Gal to see if he looked like he wanted to run but his eyes were bright an wide open an starin at the yellow front of the train that was draggin mibbi a Thirty-Sixer at least. I never bothered him in case he never wanted to run. The noise was now that loud that he'd never have heard me even if I screamed. Now I kind of liked it an didn't like it at the same time. It gave me a funny feelin from ma belly to ma heart. It was worse than fear. I decided to take it square in the eyes just like Gal was doin. There was no way I was goin to miss a look at The Bricklayer no matter how scared I was.

An engine passed an you could see the noise an magine yourself under the wheels. The wheels were so close you could've reached out an touched them. Honest to God, if I had stuck ma hand out through the grass an under the fence I could've rubbed the wheels with a big stick. An the heat an the smell made you think that you were part of the train. Even in such a wee time I managed to catch a check at Gal. He was still wide in the eyes an lookin. Another engine started to pass. He must've been readin ma mind again cos he span round, put his lips right up to ma ear, an shouted,

Shit, it's two engines... that means he'll be there... The Bricklayer.

He stared right at me an I thought that he was scared. The noise of the train vibrated through ma belly. It came right through the ground an into your body tryin to shake you right off that hill. I grips the strands of grass an Gal looks at me wonderin what the hell I was doin. It didn't bother him that much cos this is when he got sneckled in so as to get a good look at The Bricklayer's puss. I never expected the thing that happened next. Gal seemed that cool as if nothin would scare him.

I had just stopped holdin on to the grass an settled down to wait on The Bricklayer when, right out the blue the bold Gal screams. Twelve wagons had went by cos I was countin them an that's how his scream really gave me a right fright. I still hadn't seen the end of the train where The Bricklayer would be standin with both hands loaded with half-bricks an a pile at his feet.

Well! He was a couple of feet in front of me an all the fear that I was keepin down came up from ma toes an I bounced up screamin as well. I knew I was doin it but I couldn't stop. I magined the eyes drillin into ma back as I tried in to accelerate downhill. I couldn't get goin fast at all an Gal seemed to be gettin further away from me. I started cryin an runnin an even though he never turned round he slowed down a bit until I got to the speed I liked. I was waitin for a brick to smash ma head in. I kept duckin an hopin that one didn't flit over ma head an kill Gal. How would I tell that to his Maw an Da?

Oh Mister and Missus Gal your Gal got his head stoved in wi a brick that was travellin like a rocket... Right yar!

As I sped up I thought of how I'd miss the look into The Bricklayer's eyes. I know it sounds mad but that's just what I thought, that's how I member it so good. I'd've looked in his eyes. I know I would have. I mean when I looked in his eyes I'd've been scared. I'd've been a lot more scared than I was when Gal ran. Sometimes I like bein scared. Actually the only thing that I am REALLY scared of is heights... an Strangler Joe. I always go up heights an all, specially if Gal goes up them first. I like the bit where ma feet tingle an I go dizzy. It's somethin like when we were lyin lookin under the wheels of that movin train an its noises were rattlin in your ear like gettin rolled down a hill in a barrel. Man I must be mental right enough doin things that I'm scared of. If I said to Gal away at the beginning that I was scared of some things, it would be OK cos he never says anythin to anyone else that's scared. But I never said nothin to him so I just keep kiddin on that I'm not scared an he keeps on thinkin that I'm not an that's that. But I think he knows about heights cos every time we're up them his voice changes an he moves slow an tries not to do anythin jumpy. Anyhow. We're runnin down the hill terryfied.

One thing about me an the Gal, when we ran down hills we always ran down sideways. Oh we knew how to run down hills all right. People used to stare at us amazed at how we could run down hills. Even when they shouted at us an called us a pair of tubes an stuff we knew that they were really amazed at us. See, ma Da was in the army an he used to teach the rest of the army how to kill people without any gun or knife or anythin. An he said that the most important thing in the army is knowin how to run down a hill sideways. After I knew Gal a long long time I let him know how to run down the hills an some other stuff. I told him the same time we made up all our plans for gettin out of a sticky situation. But I never showed him how to kill people without a gun cos ma Da told me never to show nobody. Me an Gal showed each other what to do all the time, we were good pals that way an all. We shared everythin. You'd think we would never be parted. If you never had to get married an that I really think that me an Gal'd be pals for ever. That's not to say that we never fought. Man we had some great fights so we did. The two of us could fight just about the same but I was a wee bit better than him on account of ma knowin how to kill people without a gun an all that stuff that I never showed him.

Sometimes we'd fight every day for ages an then we would stop for a long time an then we would fight every day for ages again. We never really wanted to fight so sometimes they'd be rubbish fights an hardly anybody would watch an we would be left rollin about in the grass with a couple of people talkin away an half watchin us. It was really his big brothers Pluff Gal an Jim Gal that made us fight. They always wanted him to win. I always won. Honest. Sometimes Jim Gal'd boot me an that but the worst time was when he kicked me right on the face. The whole world flashed in front of me an I could hear myself cryin in the distance. It was weird. One of these days I'm goin to get him for that but he's mental. He only kicked me like that once but I'll not forget it; it was the time I took a krazy an couldn't stop bangin Gal's head off the kerb. He was covered in blood. It's funny. It's like up heights, I kind of liked it an didn't like it at the same time. We never really had a fight after that.

His Maw an Da battered lumps out Pluff Gal an Jim Gal for gettin Gal done in. Even all the hundreds of times that we fought, one thing for sure, we never fought when there was nobody else there to egg it on. Never.

In here quick Gal shouts as he jumps into a hollow in the rocky slope runnin down to The Burn. Boy had we travelled. I dived in as geme as I could. As I lay beside him in the rock the train passin through the trees above made everythin go

dark,

light,

dark,

light.

Man I'll tell you, that was spooky all right, specially in The Valley. There was that many trees that it was always kind of dark an the air was always wet an cold. But this time, with us scared an the train blockin out the sun an the darkness in The Valley it made us feel as if we'd done somethin wrong.

The train was way above us. We must've ran down hundreds of feet. It felt like that anyway. But the thing that Gal never seemed to think about was the well-known fact that The Brick-layer could chuck a rock for miles so we were just as daft lyin there as we were up right next to the train. I never told him in case I had to take ma face out of the dirt. It's really hard to talk with your face pressed into the ground. One good thing was that the train wheels couldn't suck you in so far down the hill. That meant that we wouldn't have to hold on to anythin an everythin to stop the suckin in.

The branch of a tree cracked above us. You could hear it right above the clackerin of the train an the way we were breathin.

We stopped breathin an crushed our heads round to look at each other. We always done a that-was-close look when somethin like that happened. This time it really was close. The brick thunked into the ground just down the hill from where we had our heads dug in. You could hear it rollin an then silence

an then

splash into The Burn.

That was a brick.

Even though I knew it was a brick I still felt good that Gal knew exactly what it was. It made me feel safe. But he was still starin at me in the noise of the train so I opened ma eyes wider to let him know that I was waitin on him sayin somethin else. He got dead excited.

This is it. This is the real thing. The Bricklayer is tryin to kill us.!!!!

The word

Bricklayer

went into ma head an made me dizzy an sick an the noise of the train was in ma bones an shakin them. The slope of the hill got steeper an steeper, it was weird. I was hangin on to stop me fallin right down into The Burn, the whole world was spinnin slow then faster an faster, like a helicopter with only one thing on it.

Hey, you look dead white.

I breathed an breathed so that Gal'd know there was somethin wrong.

Bring yer knees up to yer chest, that's how to stop that. I seen it in the Chapel. Margaret Irvine fainted an Miss Boswell made

28

her put her head between her legs. Five minutes an she was out at communion no problem.

I done it. It made me feel good an the world stopped spinnin.

Over a bit an down the slope six bigger boys were runnin. I could see some red and yellow jumpers an hear parts of their voices bouncin off the steep sides of The Valley. I thought they sounded sort of scared. They were. They were runnin across the slope of the hill an down. They ran forwards without lookin back an sometimes you could hear that they were screamin. You could tell that they were runnin away from somethin cos they were all pullin each other's Sloppy Joes an tryin to get in front of each other. I risked puttin ma head a bit higher an saw them grabbin each other an wrigglin like a tin of worms to be at the front. They were just a lot of legs an screamin voices. It was obvious that no one had ever showed them how to run down a slope before. Me an Gal would have tanked them no bother. An another thing. This grabbin each other back. Me an Gal never grabbed each other back. We done a lot of things but I can't member ever grabbin each other back. That wasn't right. I mean magine it was Bible John or Strangler Joe or somebody an you grabbed your pal back an he got caught an got choked. How would you tell that to their Maw an Da? I hated when you were with someone over The Orchard or somethin an they grabbed you back an you got caught. A lot of people done that but, as I said, me an the Bold Gal, we never.

A brick came crashin down through the trees again. One of the six boys stopped an shouted up at The Bricklayer. You could hear what he said loud an quiet comin up the hill into the train racket.

Big fat bastard Bricklayer... you're gonna get it... Cadzow Boot Boys ya Bass.

He showed his teeth an stuck his two fingers up right violent. That frightened me for two reasons.

1. He might make The Bricklayer mad.

2. He was in the Cadzow Boot Boys an they took our money off us all the time.

Oh, an another thing, now that I member, the one that shouted up at The Bricklayer, that was Duffy an he was pure mental. I heard that he got flung out St James's primary for kickin the Teacher on the leg. A right nutcase. His Da used to fight all the time at Mitchell Street an his Maw ran away with the gypsies. Ma Maw told me that. Anyway, The Bricklayer must've heard Duffy cos you just seen his red Sloppy Joe sinkin into the ground as another brick came whizzin through the dark an light air of The Valley. You'd've loved the noise that it made if you never knew what it was.

In ma head I kept on seein The Bricklayer's face as he wrenched the bricks through the trees tryin to kill us. I always used to think that he put notches on the wooden bits of his wagon every time he got somebody with a brick.

Another brick tore a big chunk out of a tree quite near us. It cracked an a white patch appeared on the trunk. I'd just noticed the noise when the white patch an hundreds of shrapnel landed on us. We forced our faces into the dirt again. Gal screamed a bit. Boy we were lucky there all right, real lucky.

It probably seems like we were in The Valley for ages with the bricks flyin about but really it only lasted a couple of minutes but it felt like ages. Me an Gal looked up an we both pursed our lips like we were goin to kiss our Grannies or somethin... we blew hard out of our tight mouths. We raised our eyebrows as we done this. We done that a lot of times when it was a really close thing. That was a really close thing. We would get about three weeks gabbin about that. Mibbi four.

I heard the other boys still runnin.

Who is that anyway? Gal asked me this so that I knew that he knew there was somebody else in The Valley. I knew that he knew cos, as I told you before, his hearin was the best in Coatbridge, easy.

It's DUFFY an that!

Gal looked at me so that I'd know that he knew what I meant by DUFFY. It meant that we weren't just hidin from The Bricklayer. Duffy was syko. Men—tal.

Another brick came through the air. This one was better. You could really hear it whirling so you could. The six boys were at the edge of The Burn decidin to jump in or not. They looked as if they were goin to lose their balance an fall right in.

This brick went whooshin through them all an socked into The Burn splashin a surprise all over their faces.

WELL!!!

You should've seen them all jumpin in The Burn at the same time.

Splash splash splash splash they went after screamin like banshees an that. Man they couldn't get in that Burn fast enough. You'd've thought that they were chasin the brick an not tryin to get away from it. They looked like a right bunch of tubes so they did. It was a laugh. Even in the water they were still grabbin each other back. I mean, me an Gal knew that The Bricklayer would never leave his train – a Captain never abandons his ship – everybody in the whole world knew that. Sometimes you could never ever make big boys out. Man they done some daft things. It was amazin they ever got to the other side of The Burn the way they were grabbin each other back an screamin like big lassies. Christ, they were nearly climbin all over each other 's backs an everythin.

See me, I've got some magination so I have. Even though I was terryfied an them boys had trapped themselves, I kept thinkin that the noise of the rocks bouncin off all the trees was thunder an the spaces in the train was lightenin. So when you looked down at the boys you thought that they were really scared of the thunder an that.

They were crushed thegether at the bottom of the big high wall into the sewer. Me an Gal knew how to get over it but you could tell that they never had a clue the way they wriggled in the same spot, like a jar of new frogs. Now they were crouchin tryin to get lower than each other an tryin to get behind each other at the same time. God they were a laugh. I mean they were the same guys that take your money off you at Mitchell Street an there they were, stuck up against a high wall, tryin to get below an behind each other. If they knew that we could see them doin that they'd kill us the next time they saw us at Mitchell Street.

That Duffy was krazy. He used to kill people an put them in the sewer so the big blades would chop you all up. BOAK MAN! Magine gettin chopped up with all the shit an piss from Coatbridge. The Bricklayer never knew who he was dealin with.

The bricks were still comin. When the guards wagon was comin towards us the brick could half you in two. Once one of the bricks went right through someone when they were playin on a swing an it was so fast that he never even knew it had happened. He never knew till he got off the swing for a draw of a fag an someone saw smoke coming out his guts. When he looked an seen a big hole right through him he dropped dead right there on the spot. Jim Gal was there an he told Gal an Gal told me, so I'm tellin you. If you ever go down to The Valley you'll know that The Bricklayer is one man not to be messed with.

You could always tell when the danger was over. The dark—light, dark—light would change to light light light an the bricks would be less feroshis. Gal tried to tell me how that happened one time but I never really listened. I should have listened. It was somethin to do with the train movin away an The Bricklayer tired throwin the bricks an he was tryin to throw them back-wards an that. I don't know. It happened anyway. The bricks were only takin little chinks out of the trees now an the light was always there.

Soon there was no bricks an the six Burn hoppers were startin to look tough again. You could hear them talkin an gettin tougher by the minute up through the new silence,

Bastard... Bricklayer... show him... he won't be back here... lucky we never got him... did you see the way I shouted at him... if he ever shows his face here again he's a dead man.

They'll be on Mitchell Street corner the night, tellin people how they nearly killed The Bricklayer only he had escaped away. Then they'll rob them of their trainers or jeans or just make them eat grass an stuff; or cardboard. They'll have dry clothes on so they won't need to tell everybody about the runnin through The Burn an tryin to get behind each other at the wall. It pissed me right off so it did. I wanted to throw a few rocks at them myself but I was too scared in case they seen me so I just lay there waitin on Gal to say somethin.

He never spoke for ages. He must've been listenin. He always never speaks for ages when he's listenin. After ma two arms had been sore with leanin on them he stuck his head up an squinted his eyes. He smelled the air to see if he could draw in any danger. I don't know why he squinted his eyes, I suppose he could listen better with them squinted.

All clear, he says jumpin up sharp an dustin the dirt an grass off his trousers. He turned to speak.

Man, that was a close shave... we really nearly got kilt there for sure.

An you knew it was The Bricklayer, Gal... shit you can listen like nothin on earth... you're a great listener...

You'd've thought that he never liked what I was sayin to him cos he turned an started headin along the hillside.

Go this way, he says.

. . . the best listener I've ever heard... so ye are Gal...

He kept creepin through the bushes. I stopped talkin an just followed him. We went that way cause it was the other way from where the six boys went but I never said, *Are we goin this way cause they boys went the other way?* or anythin. We never needed to say things like that. It was spooky sometimes. We seemed to know what we were thinkin. We were weird so we were.

Weird.

After we never heard the boys at all for ten minutes, we donnered down towards The Burn.

The Burn

Yuch!

You could taste that Burn so you could. It was mingin. Even your mouth was stinkin. Gal spat so I spat. He spat again but I couldn't cos ma mouth was dry after The Bricklayer. We came to the bottom of the slope an Gal puts his hands on his waist. I knew he was lookin for a way to cross The Burn. He listened.

His head swung to the right.

He listened some more.

His head swung to the left.

Some bits of The Burn you could jump right over in a oner. Sometimes you fell in. Other bits you couldn't jump if you were Skippy. But most of the time you never fell in. I was sort of athletic an so was Gal so we nearly never ever fell in except if you got shoved or somethin. Sometimes it was good to fall in cos it made you not care about gettin wet any more an you could walk about in The Burn havin a right laugh. You never had to be careful after you fell in an got all wet an green an slimy. You could only feel like that in the summer cos in the winter your trousers an top used to weld to your skin, it was like wearing cold cardboard, an you had to go home. You had to sneak into The House an wash your gear in the bath if you fell in in the winter. In the summer you could go to The Canal, or up The Lochs cos the water was brown there instead of green an you could wash the slime out an dry the clothes over a tree or wear them an run around like a chicken flappin your wings an that. It was a right laugh watchin somebody runnin around like a chicken tryin to dry their clothes. Sometimes, in the school holidays there was hundreds of chickens up The Lochs.

The Burn that I am always goin on about is called The Luggie.

I think that it's called that cause the person that named it seen a log floatin down an just said Luggie an that was that. I'm one for always wantin to know why things are called what they're called an that. I always want to know how things happen an that an so I ask everybody everythin.

I think your effin middle name should be Why?... Ye never stop... on an on an on an on you go Ma Da would say when I kept on askin why all the time. It didn't stop me askin questions for years an years. But after a million, *Eat your dinner an shut ups.* I stopped.

What the hell have I told you about playin down at that Burn? They'd go. Then,

SLAP!

The thing was that they usually never told you nothin about not playin nowhere near that Burn. They were always doin that, sayin they warned you about somethin when they never.

I told you that would happen... didn't I?

I can't rem...

SLAP!

I TOLD you that would happen didn't I?

SLAP!

I said I TOLD you that would happen didn't I?

SLAP!

I said I TOLD you that would happen didn't I?

Yes.

I always dropped ma head at that bit an walked out of slappin range. Ma ears would be singin to me an I'd walk away wonderin who was mad. Did they really tell me an I forgot, or was it all lies so that they could get a good excuse for slappin me right on the lug? I talked to Gal an he says that his Maw an Da done the same thing to him. Mibbi it's a game that big people play... like when you twist some body's wrist an ask them who is The King. I mean I could member some things like I was really there an I don't ever member anybody, in ma whole life tellin me not to play down at The Burn... nope... I'd've membered for sure. It always made you want to turn round an say, in a posh voice,

Look here my good man... you have never ever told me not to play down at the Burn at any time in my life!

But you knew that would get you a right good slap from your Maw an another few right good slaps from your Da when he got in from work. You always got a slap on the dish for somethin that they say is cheek. An the thing was... if I was tryin to be cheeky I could sure do a lot better than that. Anyway, it wasn't the slappin an the sayin that they told us things that they never what bothered me the most. It was them sayin that we were playin down at The Burn.

PLAYIN!!!!?

Jesus Christ... sometimes we nearly got killed... like the time with The Bricklayer that I'm tellin you about. An hundreds of other times. I'd like to see their faces if we GOT killed then see if they'd go about tellin everybody that we were PLAYIN down The Burn. What do they think we are? It made you feel like a wane so it did... a wee wane. I mean I was nine an Gal was eight... WANES?... I don't think so. There we were nearly into double figures an they're still tryin to say that we are kids... that we were PLAYIN down The Burn.

Gal spun around quick an sharp as a Blackie broke through a tree.

A nest! I shouts. By the time I shouted I was in mid-air flyin into the bush. No messin about just right in there lookin for the nest. That was when Gal landed on me an knocked the wind right out of ma sails. The two of us crashed to the ground an the thud shook the trees all the way along The Valley. You could see them shake when you looked up after the fall. I was nearly knocked out. But cause I am athletic I could stay awake an sook in enough air to stop me faintin.

Here I was lookin right into the white roots of grass with Gal lyin on top of me. I got myself ready to shout at him. Just when I was ready to really welly it out about him landin on me without warnin he shot right into the tree pullin branches apart an searchin out The Blackie's nest. I was still goin to shout at him when I membered that he was always the one who stuck his hand in the nest to see if there was anythin in it. I left him alone an waited. He was the one who stuck his hand in cause I never liked heights much an he climbed all the trees to look for nests. I'd've stuck ma hand into any nest... I wasn't scared... even a Hawk's or a Crow's... but Gal climbed the trees so it was only right that he should be the one to stick his hand in the nests. The reason I never thought this time is cause it was only a bush. Gal must've thought that I'd've tried to get to the nest before him an stick ma hand in. Well I suppose that's why he nearly killed me tryin to get to the nest first. That was his job.

I stood up an watched him. It was good havin a pal like Gal. You should've seen the way that he separated them branches. Man he was like a dancer, or like a Karate expert. Both his palms of his hands were facin away from each other as he parted an searched, parted an searched. I really liked when he done that. He really looked like he was the only boy in the world that could separate an search right so he did.

Then, he separated this bit with more care than ever. He turns to me an, screwin up his face an especially his eyes, he shoves his hand down into the bush, right up to his soldier. He wriggles it about a little mumblin to himself but still sort of lookin at me. It was great the way he done that.

He never flinched, but I jumped back an landed on ma bahookie when the female Blackie ran away from the nest screamin like a girl you just kissed. When I stopped crawlin backwards I looked up at Gal hangin there in the bush like a mountain climber. He looked more intent now. I was proud of him. He knew his job. I mean he knew that the female Blackie was goin to fly out any minute. I knew that too but that never stopped me from jumpin backwards an fallin on ma bum. So when he was shovin his hand into the bush, he never even stopped when the female Blackie flapped out crackin twigs as she went. His face was even more screwed up now. That usually meant that he could feel the rim of the nest. You could smell the warm inside, soft an secret.

He was standin on one leg so that the spring of the bush was the only thing holdin him up.

Two Blackies were spinnin round in the stinky air of The Burn. Man they were screamin their heads off. The noise bolted through the woods an down The Valley. You found it hard to tell between the birds an the echoes. Then the two of them landed on The Pipe an sat silent for a couple of minutes. They drew us some right dirty looks. They looked like their wee yellow eyes would pop out an hit me in the face. If they had done that for no reason an Gal wasn't there I'd've been scared. An a funny thought came to me. What if the birds had seen Strangler Joe? What if they knew who he was an all that? What if they seen him chokin that wee boy? Man they were evil lookin things when you thought that kinda stuff.

Whaaaaaaaaaaaaaaaaaaaaaaaaaaaaaa they jumped back into the air an screamed an screamed. Gal worked on. They never bothered him an iota, he just stretched an stretched hopin to arrive at the hard heat of the eggs.

Even though I wanted the eggs a lot I still felt kind of sorry for The Blackies. It was the kind of thing that I was never too sure to tell at confession. So I never bothered. Just stealin milk an swearin... the usual. *Bless me father for ma sins are just the same as the last time I saw you*, I'd go. He'd mumble and hit me with Ten Hail Marys an Ten Our Fathers. Sometimes I'd just sit there an say no prayers. I thought you'd've felt bad for not sayin the prayers The Priest told you to, but you never. The quiet bigness of the chapel an the murmurin oul women was good, in fact, the amazin thing is... I felt better if I just sat there an stared an missed out most of the prayers. Anyway, I'm krazy, ma mind is always wanderin. Imagination it is.

Gal was nearly there I could tell cos his silence got quieter an he was only breathin the air that he needed too. He told me that. He said, *I only breathe the air that I need too so that I don't waste ma concentration when I'm listenin for trains or spottin nests or feelin for eggs.*

Some man the Gal. I never told him that I felt sorry for the

birds an thought that you need to go to confession cos of it.
There's some things that you don't say to other boys. Even Gal.

Any in it Gal?

I asked him in the low voice I always used when I asked him if
there was any in it. Ma eyes widened so that he knew that I was
waitin for an answer. He was right in the bush now so that I
could only see half of his body an his face. I member thinkin that
his eyes were connected to his fingers cos I was lookin right into
them but he couldn't see me. He was lookin at the eggs in the
nest with the tips of his fingers. He'd be all right, the Gal, even if
he went blind. He was makin a picture of the inside of this nest.
But this time it was weird. It was like all the other times he had
seen the inside of nests with his fingers but somethin wild was
happenin now. I stared hard into his eyes. They were blue like
mine an The Sky. Then, a shudder went into me. I started to see
the inside of the nest an ma fingers felt like they were in there
in the warm softness searchin out the hard heat of the eggshells
too. His fingers were mine an mine were his. Our eyes were
locked thegether in one mission. I felt an egg. I really did,
honest. I felt an egg an he said,

One.

CHRIST! He paused. The pause was thick an sticky. All
noises had gone away except the rustle of the odd leaf an the
beatin of our hearts. We moved our fingers about the nest a
little. We never fought each other. I knew there was four in it.
Don't ask me how I knew but I did. Gal knew that there was four
an all but he never let on. He always kept you waitin at times
like this so I let him do it. He liked it that way. So he went on to
kid-on that he was countin the eggs as he found them. He
wanted each egg to be a triumph. It made him feel good.

Two.

Gigantic pause. I held ma breath pretendin not to be more

excited than I was.

Th...ree he said, like a Doctor.

He looked at me an I looked pure amazed. I wasn't but I just looked like that for him. I mean, even if I never got into his fingers this time, everybody knew that nine times out of ten you got four eggs in a Blackie's. It was always four eggs in a Blackie's. I let Gal make a big thing out of it but. It was good practice for when he was mibbi at the top of a gigantic pine tree with his hand in a Hawk's nest an countin his one-two-threes an stoppin for ages an ages between his words. Man that would be really amazin. To have four Hawk's eggs. You could swap one of them for a whole collection.

Four.

He shouts with the thing in his voice he kept for countin the last egg. You knew that he wanted you to look really surprised so that's what I done. Then he

done what he always does; he paused for ages again tryin to pretend he was doin somethin really important that nobody else in the whole world knew about. The same as when The Priest moves stuff about the altar after communion. I wasn't in his fingers any more so it made me not like Gal for a minute.

Grab ma hand.

He stretched out his left hand so that I could pull him out of the bush. The two Blackies were goin pure mental now. They never liked it one bit so they never. I was too interested in the eggs now to feel sorry for them so they just flapped round above our heads. If you looked up you could magine that they were Vultures right up there in The Sky. I never thought about them cos I knew that if I did I'd start to feel sorry for them an that would waste the lookin at the eggs.

I pulled Gal upright keepin ma eyes zoomed in on the space in the bush. His right hand appeared from the inner darkness. It shone more than the rest of him. I kept ma eyes on it. The two birds were screamin blue mudder now but I couldn't care if Bible John or Strangler Joe were flyin at us out of the trees. All that was there was Gal's right hand shut around the egg an the slappin of The Blackies' wings an their screamin.

I think Gal knew that I was in his fingers cos he said,
Man that was the weirdest nest I ever stuck ma hand into.
I just nodded.

He held out his hand an opened it dead slow an careful lookin at me then the egg then at me lookin at the egg, then at me lookin at him. That was the best bit. I seen the bluey egg startin to look out of his hand so I shut ma eyes for a minute so that I could get the whole egg on ma eyes at the same time. I like to do things like that you know. Like shockin myself an givin myself frights an stuff. But this wasn't really shockin myself in a bad way. This was somethin good but not as good as a Hawk's would've been.

I opened ma eyes for the shock. Gal was smilin so that his cheeks nearly stuck out more than his ears. I member thinkin another one of ma krazy thoughts at the time. I nearly always think of krazy things that I never tell anybody about. Man they'd lock me up in Hartwood or Carstairs if they knew the things that I think about so they would. So that's why I always don't say nothin about them to no one… see? But I'll tell you what I thought cos it don't matter much if you think I'm not the full shillin or anythin like that. It's not as if I'll ever meet you or anythin. Christ you don't even know the half of it! Well this is what I thought anyway.

The egg was sat there in his hand an I member a shiver in ma body. It was a nice shiver like a electric shock without the pain. All of a sudden I thought he was God an he was standin there in front of me holdin The Sky in his hand for all the Angels an

Saints to see. The whole bright blue Sky with light brown clouds an yet sort of green at the same time. It was funny. It was as if Gal's smile was the sun.

Wow. Hold on there Krazy Horse.

Some of the thoughts I have. I don't know. They seem to come right out of nowhere. I mean, normal you'd not even think to think about the likes of God an Skies an Angels an Saints all rolled into one. It was only an oul Blackie's egg. But that's the way ma brain works sometimes, honest, it makes me laugh so it does.

Our foreheads were touchin when I had that thought. I member that all right cos ma next thought, right after the one about God an The Sky, was that if Gal had Bugs they'd crawl from his head into mine.

Now see you an never touch heads with any the other wanes when you're out playin, ma Maw used to say when the was a nit scare at the school. I hated gettin Bugs. Man it was a killer. She lies you there with your head on her thighs an drags that Derbac comb through your hair. It's like getting dragged around in a fight. Then it's the nippy loashin… eeeyuk it stings an stinks. After that she clicks the rest of the Bugs to death between her two thumbnails.

I picked the egg up slow an soft from his hand. You always put your thumb on the top an your pointin finger on the bottom so that you could hold the fragile shell up to the light an see if it was cloakin or not. Only a right bad yin would take a cloakin egg. In case you don't know a cloakin egg is one with the yunk inside it. It's not like a real egg, there's blood in it. You only blew an egg if it was like the ones that you fry in The House, yellow an clear an that. You'd break a thorn from a tree an puncture

44

both ends of the egg where I told you about the thumb an the finger, then you'd blow into it until all the stuff came out the other end. It was horrible if you made the head of a Yunk puncture through covered in blood an wrigglin. It made me feel right sick once when I blew this egg, a Stukkie's an all I seen was this head an the wee eyes askin me, *what are you doin what are you doin. It's too early. It's too early*. I felt like a mudderer. The worst thing was that I had to crush it into the ground with ma heel to put it out of its misery. I never want to put anythin out of its misery again that's how you should always check your eggs for cloakiness.

Anyway, I couldn't tell if this egg was cloakin so I held it against ma cheek. I liked to do that. I liked the warm feelin an the smoothness. Another thing I liked was the fact that I could crush the thing if I wanted too. I never crushed an egg apart from that one that was cloakin but it was good to know that you could if you wanted.

Gimmie the thing.

Gal lifted it rough as he could without nearly breakin it.

It's a right good yin, he said again in his Doctor's voice.

He held it up to the light an screwed his face up. He could really look at an egg, in fact he could look right through an egg. He stuck it on his cheek an rolled it with the flat of his hand across to his ear. He listened to it for ages, as if he was makin sure of somethin, shook it a little beside his other ear.

Aye, it's cloakin all right. We can't take any out this nest. Let me see.

He holds the egg next to ma ear an shakes it a bit. I could hear the click-click of the Yunk's beak on the inside of the shell. It must've been right dizzy in there as we shook it about. I just knew that it never liked it. The egg was really cloakin somethin awful an, as I told you, you never take a cloakin egg.

I knew that, an Gal knew that, so we never had to say anythin about it.

The two birds were mental now all right an they were gettin closer an closer cos we were tryin to steal their children. Your Maws an Das always used to say,

How would you like it if a big giant came along an pulled you out your bed an took you away?

Now that was krazy. The chances of that happenin were a million trillion to one. Even if there is a big Giant what would he want with us? Gal stuck the egg into his right hand again. We never smiled cos this was serious stuff. We wanted the egg but couldn't take it. It had to go back. It reminded me of a funeral. Cause there were no words. All the other noises got louder an you could hear them like they were all separate instruments in a orkestra or somethin like that. It was as if The Valley was talkin to me. It had its own voice an never spoke Scottish but the mad thing was, at the time, I sort of understood what it was tryin to say to me. I never told Gal about that one either. Even The Burn smelt stronger than usual this time an I'll tell you this for nothing, that was the smelliest place in the town. The trees moved more than usual in the wind an even a car horn came down from the main road. Just then through the trees at the other side of The Burn I saw somethin move. It was a man. He was right big an he moved through the trees as if he was floatin. He turned an grinned. His grin was like a half a moon. I went to tell Gal but when I did the man was gone. Varnished. I thought it must be ma krazy magination that I told you about.

Gal gives me his left hand an tilts himself back into the bush in a oner.

Right, that's it back an the nest's still warm so they'll come back. I wonder what they'll think when they count the eggs an see that there's none missin?

Can they count?

Well they know there's two of us don't they?

How do you know that they know that?

Well.

Gal thought for a minute. He was good at thinkin how animals an stuff knew things an so was I. He got the answer first. I was thinkin about the eggs but Gal was right clever.

Got it.

I stood waitin for his answer. I liked his answers they were sometimes as krazy as ma magination. If there was somethin the Gal was good at it was answers.

Well, if I walk away from here an leave you The Blackies still won't come back to the nest. So they must know that one has went away an one had stayed. So they can count.

Wow man that's some answer so it is!!

He smiled well pleased with himself. But the eggs were still puzzlin me so I asked him another question.

Gal?

What?

Well, how do you know that The Blackies can count to four but?

Easy man... when she sits on them if she falls into the hole left by the eggs we might've took. Well? She knows there's some missin.

I just looked away. That answer wasn't as good as his other one. Everybody knew that the nest still had to be warm for the bird to come back into it. If we stayed there for the likes of half a day or somethin an the nest got freezin well, The Blackie would leave, nest the lot. We used to call that herryin the nest. You could call it herryin if you pulled the nest to bits but it really means if the birds don't go back to the nest cause of you. Nobody liked herryers. I never wanted to pass this bush the rest of ma life an know that I herryied the nest an that was even countin that I was sad cause we weren't gettin any eggs. I was a bit warm where ma heart goes when I thought of the Blackies flyin back to the nest an it still warm an that. Soon they'd forget all about us. Everybody knew that Blackies only had a memory that lasted three days. That's why they built their nests in the same mad places every year. Really, thinkin back, I don't know what all the fuss was about cos a Blackie's was the easiest egg to get. Oh… not countin chickens, they were in your Maw's press, except a Wednesday when she was skint.

We fixes up the bush so it looks like nobody's been there. If anyone seen the hole in it they'd know there was a nest in there an it would still be our fault. Gal knitted a few of the twigs thegether so it would be hard to get them opened at that bit. It was his mark that tyin-the-twigs-thegether stuff. He always done that an sometimes a whole week later we would come by a bush or a tree or somethin an the twigs would be tied thegether an we would just smile at each other like it was the biggest secret in the world. I know I'm sayin he always done that but he never if he was up a big high tree or in a wall or a factory roof. I mean… c'mon! how d'you expect a guy like Gal to twist them big branches thegether that you get up the top of some trees? You'd need to be Superboy or Desperate Dan's son or somethin to do that.

I bet that if he could the Gal fella would've done it. Man he'd've branches tied in big trees all over The Sky. An all the folk would stand there scratchin their heads an askin what it was all about. An me an him would swagger past an look at the tree then at each other an we would smile an that would be our secret. Them dumplins would just stare an stare into The Sky askin people goin past, Just what is this all about then? Mad Priests would shout about sinners an it's a sign from God. They'd

listen in the Chapels with their combed hair lookin at the floor,
ashamed. Me an Gal'd look at the floor but at the back you'd
see our soldiers liftin up an down cos we knew we done it. MY
GOD! we would've tied whole forests thegether just to let us
know we had been there. That's the kind of stuff we would've
done if we could. Trees would be tied thegether all over the
countryside from The Douglas Estate all the way up The Lochs.
The wireless would talk about it an then the telly man...

See! Told you I was mad as a brush. There goes that
magination of mine again. I'll tell you this for nothin, the back
of ma head's been slapped a few times for maginin out the
window in school.

WHACK!

Stop daydreamin Derrick. Go an stand out the front.
I'd drag ma feet an the inside of ma head was full of spar-
klers an big bells... Then (an you think I'm mad!) she'd shout,

Face the wall boy till I see what I'm goin to do with you!

How mad can you get? She was a stoater. She drags me out
for starin out the window an then makes me stare at the
wall! She never had a clue. I was just as good at maginin starin
at a wall as I was lookin out of the window. Sometimes when I
think about it, I think I am better at maginin at a wall. At a wall
you have to magine the whole lot apart from the sky-blue paper
that was pinned up there a hunner years ago. That could be a
Sky or under the sea or somethin. At a window there was always
things happenin to make you think. Things that you never
wanted to. Even a passin bird could whip you away from dancin

in the stars an laughin out into space.

Anyway. Gal was finished knittin the bush (to get back to ma story). He was finished knittin the bush an we walks away lookin back sly like.

Back yet?

Gettin closer.

What one?

The man Blackie.

How close?

On the bush an sniffin about right now.

We walk on kiddin on that we don't care about nothin, specially the Blackies an their nest when all the time that's the very thing we think about. All the time Gal's whisperin,

Brown one now, the Mammie Blackie. She's glidin back. WOW... see that... she dove right into the bush without lookin. Man she just folded her wings onto her back an crashed like a bullit into the darkness too see if her wanes were all right.

Gal was leanin right into me an his hand was tight round ma arm. His face was red an his mouth was as wide with a smile as he could get it. I let him haver on for a couple of seconds cos sometimes Gal liked to haver, then I asked him about the other bird.

What about the Blackie, the man Blackie, what's he doin?

There was a quiet as he looked.

He's watchin us.

I turned round. I can member bein a bit scared.

There in the distance, on the bush, the black bird stared us off. I swear I could see the yellow of its eyes openin an closin like a horrible little heart sizin us up for somethin terrible.

Hell Tar

We came to the start of The Pipeline. Man that thing just stuck itself right out of the ground as if it came from nowhere. I've been along it millions of times. It goes down The Valley an crosses over The Burn more times than hot dinners. It amazed me all ma life how that Pipe came out of nowhere. If you stuck your ear on it you could hear the water runnin through. It was thick an heavy. It was like as if it was tar, but it was sewage. I know that it must've ran underground but that never mattered. All I ever saw was the bit where it came out of the ground. Like somebody had jammed a couple of feet in there an it was suckin up all the black tarry stuff that Hell was made out of. Sometimes, if you were on your own an you tried to walk across one of the high bits you could feel the Hell Tar inside shakin The Pipe on its concrete ledge an tryin to throw you off. That's why I sometimes crawled along or walked down on ma hunkers with ma hands flat on the round Pipe. If Gal was there I never went down on ma hunkers, even if the Hell Tar was tryin to shake me off an down into the rocky water. Gal never knew about the Hell Tar. That was another thing I never told him about. He'd've told me I'm a right roaster an laughed his nut off.

The Pipe was that colour of green that makes you feel sick. It looked like they were tryin to get it to fade in with the trees. They never counted the winter when the trees were black like scribbles an the snowy Valley stuck the green Pipe out like a sore leg. You could read The Pipe like a History book cos all the gangs that were krazy since years an years ago had their names painted on it. I used to read them an pictures of the people would come into ma head. Woaw! They were scary all right. I used to watch for them all the time in the trees. Never seen them yet. Still lookin.

You know, it's amazin. There we were walkin down The Valley an all we wanted to do was play but all the time in the back of your hair you're watchin out for Duffy an his mob, The Bricklayer, Bible John, Strangler Joe an all the crazies that had wrote their names on The Pipe. It got that bad that I sometimes thought about givin the whole shebang up... you know playin an adventures an egg collectin an that... Me an the Gal used to wonder why big folks never done what we done but I guess they collected too many things to be scared of, over the years, till it was just too dodgy to go out for a roam an a ramble an that.

Anyway, right at the beginnin of that big Pipe me an the Gal had our names in black magic marker. Gal wrote them. His big brothers showed him how to write like gangs. You had to write your name in a way that scared the shit out of people when they read it. I wonder if anybody was ever scared of our name, or if some wanes might read them in the future? If you forgot who you were for a minute an looked at the names you could get a fright as if they were real Krazies' names.

You had to go under The Pipe to see our names. We done it under there for two reasons.

1. So as none of the real Krazies would see it an rub it out.

2. It was another good idea cos that meant no one would tell our Maws an Das.

The Pipe was kinda the same all the way along. It was green, with names on it an three feet wide. You could walk on it, like I said. It was no bother to walk on it if you had somebody with you. An, you know how Burns run downhill? Well as you got further along this Pipe it got higher an higher above The Burn.

At the same time the slopes at both sides of The Valley got higher an steeper. So as you walked along you got scareder an scareder an the trees curled in over your head from the steep sides of The Valley so that it got darker an darker.

The bit where we wrote our names, under The Pipe, was like a little house. It was a den. It was the right height. Me an Gal could just stand up in it. You couldn't jump up an down or anythin like that an sometimes your hair touched off the bottom of The Pipe. The bit above us is where The Pipe disappeared if you were lookin in from the Mill Brae, which is the main road. So if you were a Polis or somethin you could only see as far as that. The older boys used to sit there, drinkin. Sometimes me an Gal'd sit there in our den an listen for hours to them gabbin all about fightin an drinkin an girls an that. We liked the bits about the fightin an the drinkin but the bits about girls were boa—rin. Me an Gal used to talk about gettin in the pub an who was the best fighter in town an all important stuff like that. I still can't wait to grow up an drink as much as I want any time I want. Gal's the same.

Most of the time we never bothered about girls. I mean we never spoke about them at all, not even in a bad way. But sometimes I used to think funny about girls but I never told him in case he thought I was soft or somethin. But, to tell you the truth... an what can you do about it... to tell you the truth sometimes, when I went past Maureen Carrick's house, or saw her, or heard her name, I used to feel right weird in ma chest an belly an that. But that's it. I don't think that counts as bein interested in girls, so we weren't really interested in girls like I said. One thing we did know. An we knew we knew this even if we never talked about it. The thing that we knew is that girls must be somethin important cos the boys on the top of The Pipe used to talk about them more than anythin else. When they done that me an Gal'd just look at the wall or somethin... just like you do when somethin dirty comes on the telly an your Maw an Da start coughin an givin it all this *D'you want a wee cup of tea then, Pat?* and shufflin about. I'll tell you this... it never changes the picture on the screen.

But them boys on top of The Pipe. You could tell that they really liked girls. They spoke about them as if they were eggs. An they weren't just any oul egg – no siree – not some oul Blackie's like we just found. Not even a stinkin Hawk's. No way man. They talked about them girls like they were Swans' eggs... Swans'... man they were against the law. If The Polis found you near a Swan's they'd lock you up an never let you out an that's if the Swan never killed you tryin to get it. The Queen owns all the Swans in the world an that was why it was dicey to take one of their eggs. I knew some guys that did. Me an Gal even held one years ago but we never took it. We put it back.

I mind me an Gal talked about it one day an he asked me for an answer. I usually asked him for answers but this time he asked me. He wanted to know what for we never took Swans' eggs even if the Queen did own them all... he said that shouldn't matter seein as how we all hated the Queen anyhow. I couldn't argue with that: everybody I knew hated the Queen. They used to fight to climb over each other to turn the Telly off at the music bit about her so I suppose I must've hated her too. I told him that the Swans were too nice to take their eggs.

What d'ye mean NICE?

I mean they're too white an good at flyin an glidin an if we took one of them eggs we would stop one of them bein born an if everybody took one there wouldn't be no Swans an we'd never know what they were like.

Gal looked at me. For a minute I thought that he was goin to tear me to shreds for talkin like a lassie but he never. He just nodded an said,

So you think we should leave them alone cos they're beeyootafool burds?

Aye... that's it.

I coughed an walked on tryin to look like I was thinkin of somethin tough.

He coughed.

Hawks are OK but?

Aye... too right... I mean Hawks... man they're ugly all right. Pot-ugly.

An that was that. Some things we could only talk about for a minute an then we never spoke any more. There I go wanderin off again. I wanted to tell you about The Pipe. At the side of The Pipe to hold it up was two concrete walls. I knew a lot about them walls. I knew they were really made of steel an the concrete held the steel thegether but Gal never believed me. I loved talkin about concrete cos ma Da used to make them kind of walls. Gal hated me talkin about them an used to call me **a liar** an say I was talkin crap every time I tried to bump ma gums about concrete an steel.

The time before the time I'm talkin about I found this hammer an carried it from The Railway down into The Valley onto The Pipe. Gal kept tellin me to throw it away -it would only slow us down an we had to be able to move fast in case anyone tried to attack us. It'll only slow us down. It'll only slow us down. He kept on goin.

What if Strangler Joe tries to get us? I mean he's already done a couple of guys our age in?

Aye... what about it? Gal asked.

Well I could thunder him over the head with this hammer an then we would be safe an in the papers an on the telly an all that!

D'you think Strangler Joe's goin to let someone the height of us whack him over the napper with a hammer?

I just looked at him.

He looked at me to make sure I knew I was talkin crap. I gave him the look that let him think that I knew I was talkin crap: lip curled up to one side an one palm showin, raised eyebrows. You see, the reason I held onto the hammer was nothin to do with Strangler Joe at all. No no. I wanted it to chip bits of concrete off the wall so that I could show Gal the bits of steel that the concrete was holdin thegether. I never wanted him to know that so that's why I invented the story about wantin it to skite it over Strangler Joe's head. See me! Sometimes I can't half tell some great lies.

There we were on The Pipe an I walked on ahead. I never even thought about sinkin onto ma hunkers cos I was goin to prove somethin to Gal an I felt gigantic. When I was a good bit in front of him an he couldn't see me cos the trees were leanin all over The Pipe, I chipped away right fast at the wall till you could see bits of thick, rusty steel wire lookin at you. It seemed to take me days an he was stopped down The Pipe a bit listenin for different birds an countin wagons on distant trains.

By this time I had seen enough metal and I could shout on Gal. The sweat was runnin out me so it was runnin out like water. For a minute I never knew if the rushin noise was The Burn below, the wind above or the sweat runnin out ma body. Ma face was purple when I shouted on him. As he wrestled through the trees I had another swipe at the chunk. Man it's a wonder, thinkin back now, that The Pipe never fell down; the amount of concrete I rattled into The Burn.

Gal arrived. He knew ma game now but never let on. He gave me that what-is-it? look. So I played just as well, caught his eyes with mine an swivelled them round an down to the bit of missin

wall. When I felt his eyes lookin I kinda polished the bit of steel
with a licked finger. I tilted ma head to the side an grinned with
ma mouth shut – you know that there-you-are look you give to
people when you've proved your point. Boy was he mad.

Aye... right yar he said.

I was ragin now. He always done that when he never believed
you. He had a right-yar look too: he'd twist his ear an stick his
tongue out at you as if his ear was connected to his tongue.
Once he seen the madness on your face he'd wind his tongue
back in an skip away laughin. That's what he done that time. I
mean there I was provin that the wall was made out of steel an
he still wouldn't believe me. What have you got to do to make
someone believe somethin that they don't want to? Who
knows?

I points at the steel an shouts down The Pipe to him,

*Look ya doob... howd'ye think they hold up The Pipe? There's
tons an tons of the stuff in there... What d'ye think they put it
there for?... I mean... for... for... for...*

On an on I shouted an all I could hear was ma voice echoin
about The Valley an his feet clickin off The Pipe an gettin further
an further away.

I ran.

No hunkers nor nothin.

When I reached him I grabbed his soldier an span him round.

How d'ye think they hold The Pipe up then? Eh?

Cement!!

he says an walks off again. He knew that would get me mad. It
was concrete an he knew that I got mad if you called it cement. I

told him hundreds of times that it was called concrete but sometimes there was no tellin Gal nothin. But I tries to tell him again just in case this was the time that I got through that thick skull of his.

It's not called cement ya dumplin it's concrete...

KON...KREET.

He turns round an acts like he was born with somethin wrong with him, put on a glaykit voice:

Oh... thas light... yoo Da... he knows iffrihin... dead smart your Da...

Then he puts on a deep man's voice. He's makin me really mad now.

Listen son... Listen to yer Da... See that stuff they make The Pipe out of?

Next thing he's doin me.

Yethhhhh Daaddy.

He puts his hands behind his back an stands like somethin out of that Bambi film. Then he's doin ma Da again.

Well son... your task in life is to go out there and tell them all that it's called concrete... Knock bits off the wall if you have to but let them know that there's steel in there by the ton... an if they don't believe you son... keep tellin them till they're sick in the teeth about it all...

He walked on goin *sick to the teeth*
sick to the teeth
sick to the teeth
sick to the teeth

an I stood there wishin he was dead. I wished Strangler Joe would jump out the trees an choke the life right out him. I'd make sure that the last thing he saw was me grinnin at him an mibbi holdin up a bit of concrete an wavin it about an that. He shouts through the trees.

*Your Da knows every*thin *every*thin... *every*thin. *Every*thin.

So I yodels back through the darkenin air.

Mo... *ore* than *yoo*...ours.

I held ma hands up to ma mouth an made a kind of funnel out them so that he'd really hear me.

I do...on't think so...o.

I slagged his Da.

Tell me so...mething... Yo...our bi...ig skinny Da...a knows but mi...ines do...on't?

His head crashed through the trees. He must've ran back towards me when I was shoutin about his Da.

Fightin... That's what... Ma Da'd kill your Da. Right yar...

This time I gave him the Laurel an Hardy look.

No bother!

He sticked his chin out wantin me to go on.

But sometimes you couldn't tell him nothin. So I marched off. Hunkers were the farthest away thing in ma head. I flung the hammer in The Burn. I never even stopped to see it splashin. I just stamped along The Pipe not talkin. We gave each other the silent treatment all day that day but we never fought. As I said we only really fought when other people made us do it.

But where am I? That's another story. This is the story about what happened. I keep wanderin away. This day... you know the day that we found the Blackie's eggs! Well, that put us right in the mood for egg huntin so we walked along The Pipe lookin for nests. You could get to some right good bits for egg huntin if you went along The Pipe cos the birds only stayed away from roads an paths an that... you know the places where you always get hundreds of people passin all the time.

I walked along the middle of The Pipe an was thinkin about hunkers. Gal walked on the little wall at the side. It was a right good drop from there into The Burn but he never cared. Sometimes you'd think that he wanted to fall in an die. When we came to the bit that I had chibbed out of the wall we looked at each other an laughed. We were in a good mood now. Gal took to hoppin on one leg cos he knew that would terryfy me. I never looked.

Look... look!

He kept on shoutin. I span round an for a minute I thought he had fell off The Pipe. But do you know what he done? He hung himself off The Pipe. I spotted his hands an then looked down through the gap at the bottom. You could see his feet danglin there an his laugh was mixed in with the runnin of The Burn. You could see The Burn an it made me

DIZZY.

I turned away an told him I was walkin away an if he fell no one was goin to lock me up for mudder. I mean you never know what could happen if he fell. After a couple of steps I hears him heave himself back up. Man he was mental. That might not be the worst bit of The Pipe but I'll tell you this... if he fell it would be the size of two houses an onto big jaggy rocks at the bottom.

The worst bit was when it went over the second time. The Burn wound under it a lot but the second time was the worstest. Man it used to make me right dizzy at that bit. Between The Pipe an the two walls was a space that you could look down an see the water rollin by. You really had to get on your hunkers there an stare at the green Pipe so that the water couldn't hypnotise you into it. That's how a lot of people died: the water tricked them down into it. But the thing I used to be scared of more than anythin was in case I fell down into the gap between The Pipe an the CONCRETE walls an get myself trapped by the head. Yeuch! You'd just be hangin there an you couldn't scream an you'd smell the stinkin Burn an the trees an the sewer an your feet would be lookin for somethin to get onto an you'd just swing to death. You needed to get on your hunkers there. Sometimes I don't look up at The Pipe if we're down in The Valley cos I think that one day I'm goin to see a dead body's feet danglin there away above The Burn.

I always walked dead slow where The Burn ran under for the second time an Gal'd show off even more by hoppin from The Pipe to the wall, from the wall to The Pipe, from The Pipe to the other wall, back onto The Pipe.

Sometimes he'd go from The Pipe to the wall an tilt so that he was startin to fall off. I'd feel ma heart jammin up ma mouth an he'd grab the hangin branch of a tree an spin right back up there like he never left it in the first place. Right round he'd spin in the open. Go nearly that quick that you never knew it was happenin. One of these days the branch is goin to break an he'll be lyin there where they found that laddie from Townhead choked stiff by Strangler Joe. They found him right below where The Pipe runs over for the second time.

Don't you be goin down near that sewer.

That's what ma Maw used to shout every time I skipped the fence into Gal's house.

An what have I telt you about skippin that fence. D'ye think yer Da built that for the good o his health?

I knew not to answer questions like that. I never thought why he built it. I always though that people made things so that all the other people could tell them how great they were at makin things.

An mind an go nowhere on your own.

I never went anywhere on ma own. It was always me an Gal. Gal an me. An even all the time we were up trees an down holes an on Pipes between The Burn an The Sky we always kept a lookout, like I told you, for the like of Strangler Joe.

So. There we are on this Pipe an I'm wantin to go down on ma hunkers but Gal can see me so I can't. Every ten steps there's a big lump where they joined pipes ten steps long.

They never bothered the likes of Gal but they bothered me cos I never used to lift ma feet when I walked on The Pipe. I used to slide along it as if I was ice skatin. I used to call it The Pipeline Shuffle so that it looked as if I was doin it to be geme but ma blood used to stick out ma arms every time I came to nine steps. For a second I'd have to be standin on one leg up there high above The Burn that was tryin to trick me into it. But ma feet were like two big magnets an that helped a lot. It was hard work to lift one of them off an just as you done it... clamp... it was sucked right back down again. I used to worry that before the other leg could zonk itself back onto The Pipe its pal would go a slidin down the side. Man I'd be scramblin up the side like as if it was a muddy river bank an all the time I'd be fallin down into the gap. Gal'd run at me but he'd be too late an I'd die there while he ran home to tell them I was stuck in the gap between The Pipe an the CEMENT wall. He'd get all the slaps in the head for,

Bein slap *down* slap *The* slap *Pipe* slap *in* slap

the slap *first* slap *place.* Slap.

He'd get,

What have I told yous about goin down The Valley. . . I hope you never crossed that railway.

Then,

How many times... blah... blah... blah.

An while they slapped him about an got him to repeat the story a million times I'd be hangin by the neck in the gap an ma feet would be lookin for somewhere. Aye... they'd be sorry when they got there an the only thing movin was ma laces blowin in the wind an The Burn below.

I reached another lump in The Pipe an cause I was extra scared this day I wanted to belly flop along it but Gal would have slagged me for years an years for that one so I just lifted the oul magnets an said a Hail Mary that the other one wouldn't run out of force before its pal clamped. There I was shufflin along between lumps an dreamin away.

Are you wantin to rub all the paint off this Pipe or something?

You know I always do The Pipeline Shuffle Gal... I'm tryin to get all the way along to the sewer without even liftin ma feet once. Apart from the lumps... You're allowed to do that...

That right? Well.

He hooks ma eyes this time an swishes them down to his one leg. He's holdin his other leg with his hand like he's a one-legged pirate. I looks at him.

I've been hoppin the whole lot since away up there where it goes over for the first time!

Man I was amazed at that. No fear. I kidded on that we were both krazy an ma shuffle an his hop were the best thing since sliced loafs. He fell for that one. He always fell for it easier if he was to be a hero in it. Most people will fall for anythin so long as you make them think that they're great. Don't get me wrong now, Gal was great with the hoppin an all that. I never wanted him to notice that I was terryfied. It worked.

The real truth of the matter is even though I'd been on that Pipe hundreds of times there wasn't one time that I really wanted to be there. I would have rather walked away round the long way. Every time I was on it I wanted to get off it as quick as I could. That's why I was really glad when Gal stopped an stared at a tree that was near to The Pipe. I knew he had a plan. He was lookin the same way he always does when he's got a plan, you know pressin his lips tight, closin his eyebrows a bit an noddin his head up an down. I know he stole that one from the telly but he was so good at it I never let on that I knew. He was checkin the branches with his Indian look now like he knew all about trees. For a minute I thought he was goin to bust into song specially for the tree but he never he just turns to me, Right, I've got a plan.

See! I knew he had a plan. Sometimes you could tell what Gal was up to before he could. I kidded on that I was real interested but.

A plan? I asked him makin him feel that he was givin me a great Christmas present. He looked back at the tree in silence so that I'd guess the tree was part of his plan. He stares up the slope into the black bits between the trees.

We want up there in the woods behind the sewer... right?

That was a question you could answer but only if you said yes. It was somethin like them questions that I told you about...

You know, *How many times have I told you not to go down that Valley?* Only this question had an answer:

Aye.

I said it slow that on way you say things when you want the other guy to know that you are wonderin. I was wonderin what his plan was that's why I said it dead slow... almost like I was born talkin like that. I never knew that we wanted to be up there in them woods. I never even knew what we wanted to do up there but I just nodded away like a lost puppy an agreed with him an his plan. He still stares at the forest an then back to the tree that was next to The Pipe.

His plan was startin to make itself up in ma head. I started to not like what I was tellin myself. Ma eyes jumped onto the tree, bounced back to Gal, down to ma magnets an then poinged over to the gap between The Pipe an the tree. Oh man I never liked it. I never like it one bit. The gap was about the size of me an gettin bigger by the second. He turns to me right cool an says,

All we need to do then...

His body turns toward the tree. I knew it! I knew it! Ma body starts to go down on its hunkers automatic so I makes like I'm fixin away at ma shoes.

Is jump into that tree...

That was the words I never wanted to see comin out of his mouth. It was right spooky. There was times when I knew exactly what he was goin to say. I can't stop it. His plan comes gushin out all over me.

... there an climb down it to the ground so that we can sneak up the hill without the Workies seein us. We'll sneak up there behind the Workies' hut. There's no way I want them catchin me. They'll throw us into the sewer an we'll get all chopped up with them big swishers an get flushed out to the sea an we'll be dead.

He was right. We all knew the Workies threw boys into the sewer. In fact just last week Tam Caddel had a amazin escape. They caught him an took him into the hut an they voted to chuck him into the swishers. They dragged him over to the edge. He peed his trousers an they let him go. Said that there was enough piss in there an they never wanted no more. So me an Gal decided that if they ever caught us, know, if we couldn't run in different ways to get away, we would piss our trousers. We never told anybody that's what we were goin to do. But that's it, you never let any other gangs know your plans so you never. He spoke an jumped me out ma head.

Right then I'll go first.

For God's sake I said into myself. I thought we would sit an talk about the plan for a wee while. I never knew we would just get right on with it there an then. Ma heart tried to escape out through ma chest. I felt dizzy but the oul magnets held me there. I felt sick so I took some deep breaths. I felt sicker so I held ma breath. Gal walked onto the edge of The Pipe.

It's no problem.

He's jumpin when he says them words. Ma heart stops. It's too quick to scream so I let it fall back into ma belly. He grabs out of mid air an catches a branch. Ma heart starts again. He swings his feet up an laughs. Ma heart stops again cos I know I've to do it. Ma heart never liked it one bit. Not one bit did it like it. No sir.

Hahahahahahahahahahahahahahahahahahaha.

His laugh bounced around the place. The Workies must've heard it. I pretends to walk onto the concrete an slip.

Are ye OK? he shouts up to me.

Aye Gal ma man, I just slipped… thought I was down the gap there.

I said that as tough as I could so that he never knew I was scared of the jump. Well it wasn't the jump that terryfied me. It wasn't the grabbin onto the branch at the other end either. What was the worst was the hangin there in mid air after you jumped an before you got the tree.

C'mon... get yersel up on the cement bit an I'll show you what to do.

I never bothered about him callin it cement. This was serious stuff. Names never mattered. I mean the stuff the wall's made out of could be called shkplmph an it would only matter for arguin. It would still be the same stuff; another name wouldnae make it different. I starts to move. Ma whole body tingles. I plucks the magnetic feet off The Pipe one at a time till I find myself perched on the concrete wall. I'm holdin on with both hands an feet. Slowly I straighten up. I went as slow as I could. Ma arm goes out like a ballet dancer automatic. It was some drop. I nearly fell off when I looked down. I nearly gave up an shouted on ma Mammy. I want to burst out greetin but I nicks it in time. Gal's gettin further away by the minute. I'm doin ma shuffle along the wall but you never felt as safe with just the steel inside the concrete to pull at your magnetic feet. It was too hardto magine. Gal looks over at me tryin to encourage me with his face. I felt like a cat up a tree. He knew I wasn't shufflin along in a daydream now. I'm like a Meccano man an white as the inside of a frog. I gets to the bit across from the tree. That's when I know there's no way I'm ever goin to jump. The devil himself couldnae get me to jump. Gal's face tries harder.

It's easy. Just jump an grab this branch here.

He waves a branch about as if he's throwin me a rope an I had fell into the sea. The branch is movin from side to side. God was I dizzy now.

It's only easy cos you are over there Gal.

I think I was kind of cryin there at that bit; not unless there was an insect on ma cheek slowly crawlin down. I member I wanted him to come across an cuddle me. I know that sounds sissy but that's what I wanted him to do. I stopped tryin to kid on I was brave.

Derruck... look... jump... grab the branch... that's it.

I decided to turn back an tell him to get me at The Hotel. I looks behind me to see if I can put the magnets on The Pipe without fallin down the gap.

Up The Pipe in the scrunched trees somethin's movin through at me. It could be anythin. That meant I'd have to go the other way an try to dodge the Workies. The trees burst open. Shit! A big tall skinny man. Like him out of Syko. Walkin so fast that he's runnin with his legs straight. He's all dressed like a Coffin Carrier. He catches his black hat as a tree tries to knock it off. His face is white. Man I'll never forget that face. It was pure white like he had painted it with door paint but his eyes were yellow. He grins an his body stretches out to the sides so that he's coverin The Pipe an the two concrete walls. He comes at me. He was no Workie. I can see his eyes. His head's swingin around madly to see if there's anyone about. He was so close I could see his brown teeth. Man I swear I could smell his breath. Just then he trips over one of the lumps.

I don't know how it happened cos there's me in mid air. The skin on ma face is stretched dead tight. I can feel it pullin ma lips back the way dogs do it. Ma eyes are tryin to get wider than ma mouth. I'm catchin flies in ma eyes they were that wide. I looks at ma hands. They're too small to go round the branch. Gal's face is solid. You can see he was wishin me across that gap. The branch got thicker an thicker. I thought I was goin to grab onto it an slide right back off again. Then, I'm swingin from the branch the way Gal done it. It never seemed as scary as I'd thought. I lets out a Tarzan call. I had to swing ma legs up a couple of times till I got them over the branch.

A doddle... no problem.

I was purple with fear an happiness. But at the same time as tryin to kid Gal on that I wasn't scared I looked up to The Pipe expectin to see that man flappin his arms thegether like a crow, or starin at me evil like. Nothin. Not a thing. Only the whistlin birds an the wavin trees an the smell of The Burn mixed in with the smell of the sewer. I decided not to tell Gal. I should've told him but I decided not to in case I was just goin bonkers for a wee minute.

The Workies

Apart from the man, I felt great now. I had jumped the most dangerous jump ever an could boast about it for ever. Gal never mentioned how scared I was either so that was somethin good. He was good at that was Gal. He never ever cast it up when you were slaggin him in front of people nor nothin. He was some man. It was good to have a pal like that. Don't think that I'm a sissy or somethin. I mean I don't go round sayin how good Gal is all the time. But to tell the truth after the fright on The Pipe an the guy I thought I saw there was only one other person in the whole wide world that I wanted an that was ma Maw. Anyway sometimes he was great. That's it, that's all I'm sayin.

Ye OK?

He looked right into ma eyes an hooked into ma brain. I never said nothin but he knew what I meant.

C'mon.

He scoots down the tree an I follows him. Man it had been some day so far. I liked it when the days were like this. Even if you're the most terryfied you've   been in months. Great! It made you feel like a boy in a comic.

Shhhh! The Workie'll hear us.

He slinks down onto his hunkers an starts to listen.

What'ye listenin for Gal?

I whispered at him with ma neck stretchin ma head out towards him. He looked at me like I should know what he's doin.

To see if they're all out in the sewer or in the hut playin at cards. They do that all the time. When there's no shit or piss comin down The Pipe they take a break an go in the hut an play at cards an eat their piece an drink their tea till we all start goin to the bog an all the stuff comes trundlin down The Pipe.

Yeeuch! Imagine eatin a piece in a sewer... that's mingin

man... pure mingin. That'd make ye sick as a pig so it would.

Aye, well, ye can only get a job here if ye can't smell an you're not scunnered by the sight of shit an piss all over the place... plus the odd dead dog... all the chopped up seagulls an the wee guys they've chucked in over the years.

They never chucked Tam Caddel in!

He's a wee liar... they ALWAYS chuck ye in!

Well I met him an his trousers were pissed... an...

Gal jumped right in, What day was it?

How?

Just tell me... Was it a Wednesday?

Aye... yer right... it was. How did ye know that?

His Da gets his Bru money the same day as mine an he drinks an chases wee Tam round The House with a big belt so that's how he pisses his trousers. He does it all the time in school on a Wednesday cos he's scared to go home.

I thought about it. I membered seein his Da drinkin with Gal's Da. He frightened me so mibbi it was true, mibbi no one's ever left the sewer alive if they got caught by the Workies.

I'd not work here for all the tea in thingway...

Gal looked at me, shook his head, All the tea in China... China.

Oh... aye... that's right. All the tea in China.

He goes silent an starts to listen again.

Are they in the hut? I asks him poppin ma head up to see if I can see anythin movin about. There's the thrum-thrum of the big machines that drive the swishers an the gurglin an whooshin of water. It's like bein inside a washin machine.

I think they're in the hut right enough. I can't hear no footsteps so they must be in there playin at cards an drinkin their tea... Right are ye ready?

Wait a minute.

I gets ready to make the dash across the road. I done that by gettin into the position them sprinters get into on the Lympics. Gal looked at me as if I was daft but I was the fastest runner in Cadzow. I used to go runnin for miles an miles just for the hell of it. I'm mad sometimes so I am.

Are you ready?

Aye.

I tried to relax but I couldn't. Ma muscles were solid.

GO GO GO

he screams an rushes across the road. All I could see was his bum goin from side to side an his elbows jaggin up into the air.

WHAM.

I was right beside him even before I knew I was runnin. He flings himself into the long grass at the other side of the road. I land beside him with a thump that near knocks me out. It winded me so I couldn't talk. He wasn't talkin cos he was listenin again so we just lay there with the wind movin the grass about just above our heads.

I sort of liked lookin at the grass, like as if all the clocks in the world stopped an all the cars an that. Like that film about the world standin still an me an Gal lyin there lookin up an gettin our breath back. All I could see was the gold grass tops an the blue Sky fluffed all over by white clouds as if God had been sleepin an his pillow burst. I know I'm krazy sometimes but at that time, you know, when the world stopped, there was no sewer, no man on The Pipe, no Pipe, no Bricklayer or Bible John or Strangler Joe. It was like it was only me an ma Gal in the middle of a big field full of corn an we had nothin to do an, anyway, all we wanted to do was lie there an watch the clouds makin shapes at us.

We watched the clouds an the stars a lot me an Gal so we did. We would lie flat on the ground an just look out there into Space. You couldn't see Space in the daytime but you still knew it was there. Any time there was anythin on about Space I watched it on the Telly. The Tetley tea used to give you a card about Space so I drank hunners of tea an got ma Maw to buy the same kind all the time. I asked anyone that came in to The House if they wanted tea... even the debt-collectors.

I used to wonder everythin about the Stars. What they were an that. I was right interested in the likes of the Solar System an all that, the Universe. I used to tell Gal all the planets an he loved it. I loved tellin him. It made me feel big but that wasn't why I loved tellin him. I think it was cause I wanted him to come out into the Universe with me so that we could get that feelin thegether. I knew all the Planets an the names of all their Moons an that. Gal always got me to talk about the Asteroid Belt. We knew there was somethin funny goin on out there. I swear it me an Gal knew that them Spacemen were ready to talk to our planet. It's hard to tell how we knew but you can believe this if you like, me an him were the ones they'd've talked to if they came that year. We were on the right tuner for them man. Every night, specially if we saw somethin movin up there in the glassy stars, we would be sure that this was The Night, in fact every night we went back home surprised that they never came.

I just knew there was somethin lookin at us, that there was somethin funny goin on out there that we never knew about. I knew that without readin it in any books or seein it on the telly; I never asked nobody about it, I just knew there was somethin strange about the whole thing. Even when them Americans landed on the moon before the Russians, that was never a big thing to me like it was a big giant thing to all the other folks about. I mean what's so amazin about that? The moon was only across The Burn really. Compared to me an Gal's eyes landin on the stars, landin on the moon was like gettin a bus into Glasgow, that's all, a bus to Glasgow. Not that I wasn't interested in it. I was. I never took ma eyes off the telly when they went to the moon. I wanted them to do more but. I wanted them to try to hit that golf ball right off the moon an send it skimmin through space so that some other planet, or wanderin spaceman, would find it an then find us an then mibbi me an Gal'd get our chance an talk to them first cos we were always lookin out to the stars an shoutin,

Can you hear us out there?

an waitin for an answer.

We never got our answer yet but we still knew they were there, they were listenin. We still knew they could hear us man. Don't ask me how we knew they could hear us we just knew that someone was listenin that's why we kept on lookin an shoutin. I don't know... mibbi it was God or somethin.

Gal poked his head up above the grass an checked that everythin was OK. It was. Once he had stuck his head up there for a bit an looked here an there, I decided to stick ma head up. I done it the way they do it in the war in case any mad snipers got the sights locked onto the grass tops an **shzzwing** you're a dead man. *Achtung Engländer! Gott in Himmell* an all that stuff. The tips of the grass tickle ma cheek bones an ma head turns like it's a machine. No one was movin about so I waits to see what Gal is goin to do next. He flops down on his belly an makes like a commando through the grass. He slithered so good that he was out of sight in seconds an all you could hear was the swish-swish every time he pulled himself along by the arms.

Do this till we're well away from them Workies' huts.

He whispered that through the swish-swish an movin grass. I starts to slither. He was a better slitherer than me but I started to do it anyway. I never wanted to stick ma head above the grass an anyway him with the black on that was on The Pipe; him that I told you about, he kept comin back into ma head an his grin the size of a half a bin-lid terryfied me no end so it did an that was just thinkin about him. It never mattered that Gal was a better slitherer than me cos I was up there beside him in no time. He must've slowed right down to let me catch up. We were side by side slitherin up the long slope of the hill towards the whizzzzzzzzzzzzzzzzzzzzzzzzzzzzzzz of the cars on the road above. We're makin two lines in the long grass an the grass between us looks like a curtain. I could see Gal mysterious like I was lookin through a fog that had been painted between us by somebody that never painted right an used straight lines instead of swirls an that. He caught me lookin at him, likin the way he could slither. He nods an points hard twice to tell me that we we're movin ahead an up. We slithered up that slopin hill man like two slugs. Our bellies never left the ground an we reached the metal fence.

Thegether.

The Golfie

We must've been stoatin about them woods for hours an we never had no luck with the eggs. Once Gal ran down to the roots of a big tree that had been blew over in the gales. We thought it was a Wren's but there was nothin in it an then we weren't sure if it was a nest. That was when I seen him again. I looks down at the road we had crossed after we slithered to the top of the hill an I seen him clamberin over the fence. His hands were locked in the flat gaps between the metal spikes. He looked like Hen Broon only he was scary man. He was grinnin up at me, like he could see right through the trees.

Gal, look at that man down there...

Where?

He swings his head everywhere but the bit where I am lookin. I gets behind him an fits ma knees into his knee sockets so I can point his eyes at the bit I want him to see.

He lets me move him about.

There.

I points so that he could run his eye down the length of ma arm an see the man. He was still tryin to get off the fence an his grin was still starin at me. He was dressed in black right enough an that was when I knew that I never made him in ma magination.

God sakes Derruck... he's a right spooky lookin guy... know who I think that is?

Gal shivered an then so did I cos I was locked into him like Lego.

Bible John... that's who it is...

We shuddered. He was tryin to cross the road but his grin looked like it had already crossed. I talked to Gal in a half-whisper but ma eyes were still locked on to where the tip of ma finger was still pointin.

*He might be The Bricklayer an he's got off the train an he's
lookin for them that chucks all the stuff at him an he'll just grab
us an do us in an an an...*

I couldn't talk any more cos he disappeared from ma finger-
tip an walked away up the road. He never jumped the wall into
The Golfie where we were searchin for eggs an that in The
Triangular Woods. They were a patch of pine trees planted in a
triangle an you could only get into them if you were wee. You
found golf balls in there. I knew Gal was scared an that made
me even scareder. He felt me gettin scareder so he started to
talk about somethin else but it was no use cos he looked like he
turned into one of them wooden dummies the ventrilykwists use
an he was workin his own mouth from his head so that he could
think the scary things into himself.

*I know. We'll go up the library the morra an look up what a
Wren's nest looks like an then we'll be able to tell if that was one.*

He points down to the tree where we never found a Wren's
nest. He knew he never talked enough cos I never answered him
– he could still see that grin shinin in ma eyes an he knew I
wanted him to take it away, so he talked again.

*OK. We'll have to get a plan. Who says we head up The
Lochs. Pat Martin says there's a Kestrel's up there in the jungley
bit near the rubbish tip.*

That was the right thing to say cos it meant that we could get
out of them woods an head in the other way that the guy with
the bin-lid grin never went. I liked that. Gal looked at the man's
face disappearin out ma eyes an started to do a good grin
himself. I liked his grin. I ain't never seen this grin before but. It
was like the one he uses when he's got a plan but it was like he
felt sorry for me or somethin too. I never felt bad about that nor
nothin. In fact I kind of liked it an everythin in me went quiet

again an warm. Gal was good at this. He starts to talk again so that he can take me far away from that terrible face.

We're hop-skip-an-jumpin across the cushiony grass of The Golfie.

HEY YOU THIS IS A PRIVATE GOLF COURSE!

There was two rich guys away over the left wavin their golf sticks at us. We gave them the fingers an the fattest one started what he thought was runnin at us.

HEY YOU THIS IS A PRIVATE GOLF COURSE!

God ma Granny could've walked faster with me an Gal on her back. We done the stupidest run you ever seen. There we are fallin, crawlin an pullin each other back for a laugh an kiddin on that we broke our legs an all sorts. The fat guy's still wobblin at us with his golf stick in the air an glintin in the sun like that's what he's goin to kill us with when he gets us.

THIS IS A PRIVATE GOLF COURSE!

C'mon wobbly jelly man... wobbly jelly belly man... big red face like a fryin pan... combed his hair with the leg o' the chair... wobbly jelly belly man...

Man Gal could make them up on the spot.

We gave him more fingers an done The Funny Run a bit more to let him catch up so that we could make his face go redder.

JUST YOU STAY THERE YOU PAIR OF CHEEKY

LITTLE MONKEYS... NIGEL... TELEPHONE THE POLIS... WE'LL SHOW THESE TOERAGS THEY CAN'T JUST STROLL ONTO OUR GOLF COURSE AN RUIN IT.

HEY YOU THIS IS A PRIVATE COURSE!

Nigel was scared of the belly man cos he dropped his stick an ran up to the clubhouse. But they always done that. We knew The Polis would never come so we shouted over at Nigel.

Nigel... oh...NEYE...GEL.

He looked round an we gave him all sorts of abyuse. By now the fat guy thought his luck was in. He was right next to us.

STOP RIGHT THERE YOU PAIR OF WEE BISOMS.

You could tell through his puffin an pantin an rantin an ravin that he thought he just needed to walk over now an hold us till Nigel got back from kiddin on that he phoned The Polis. Then the two of them would terrorise us a bit for their own fun... the usual stuff.

I think we'll cut them up and feed them to the dogs Nigel. What do you think?

Well Victor, why don't we bury them up to their necks in the sand bunkers and then whack their heads to a pulp with these here golf clubs?

But there was no way me an Gal were goin to let them do that. We always took the mince out of them sort of guys - they might be rich but that never made them clever an we might be

poor but that never made us daft is what my Granny used to say.
He reached out to grab Gal's arm. He just stood there like he was
terryfied an the guy had him fair an square. For a minute he had
me fooled too. But, just as Fatty's hand touches his jumper he
bolts about ten feet an gives him the oul thumb on the nose
treatment. Fatty hated that. He spun round to see if Nigel was
comin back from kiddin on he phoned The Polis. He wasn't. Next
thing, he makes a dive for me. He just dove right at me. Right
off the ground he was.

Well!

Do I not just spin the other way like I'm dribblin a ball, like
Jimmy Johnstone, round Jerry Brolly an

SPLAT!!!!

there's oul Redface sprawled out on the ground. I could see
Nigel away in the distance out the corner of ma face. Gal's
behind the Fat Guy pokin at his feet an legs with the golf stick
that he dropped. He started to scream at us like a squealin pig.
He was gettin redder an redder. I though that it was time to bolt
the course now but Gal kept on proddin.

WHAT'S YOUR NAME? WHERE DO YOU LIVE? I'LL REMEMBER YOUR FACE.

He kept on repeatin all that kind of stuff an Gal kept pokin
away with that stick. Nigel was runnin an gettin closer.

Ma name is Macknemarra I'm the leader of the band...

Gal sang at the guy over an over. He managed to get onto his hunkers but you could tell he had no intention of standin up he just haunched there huffin an puffin like a big whale. Gal threw the stick as far away as he could. Man it swished through the air like a spaceship.

GAAAAAAAAAAAAAAAAAAAAAAAL! I screams.

Another two golfers were right on us. A big one with red hair, looked like a Polis, had his hand just about to grab Gal when I shouted. We were caught for sure an I was already makin up excuses an gettin glad that I never poked the guy with the stick when the bold Gal drops to his hunkers an next thing we've got three big men on the ground an Nigel gettin too close for comfort. We shoots the Craw. We never ran in different directions cos they weren't chasin us. We stands at the other edge of The Golfie an gives them The Funny Dance. They pretended to run at us a couple of times so we kidded on that we ran away but we only ducked down the back of the trees out of sight. We counted five-ten-double-ten-five-ten-a-hundred twenty times an got right back up there an shouted an gave them The Funny Dance till they got plain fed up with the whole shebang an walked away hittin their little golf balls before them.

We'll head up The Lochs by the farm right?

Gal asked this an never waited for an answer. We rustled through the trees just in case any of them golfers tried to follow us an really get The Polis. They never. Once we calmed down a bit we walked slower an looked in the bushes we passed for nests. I had nearly forgot about the man with the grin that I saw on The Pipe an the spiky fence. The bold Gal sees me gettin scared again so he tries to get me maginin other things.

What's the very first thing you member?

What d' you mean?

I knew what he meant but I wanted to see if he really wanted a big answer or if a short answer would do.

What's the very very very very very very first thing you member in your whole life?

That made it more easy: he wanted a big answer if I could get one but a short one would do if it had to.

Do... you mean the very first thing I member ever... as far back as I can go... when I was right wee?

Aye. As far back as you can member.

He leaned forward so that he was just a nose an two eyes above two flattened palms. He asked me,

I mean... can you member ever bein in a pram?

Hmmmmmmmmmmmmmmm... no not a pram but...

Can you ever member gettin your nappy changed?

Nope but I can member...

Can you ever member sookin yer Maws diddies?

Och GAL... you're a clat!! . . . What are you talkin about now?

The thought sent shivers up an down ma back. Not the scary ones like him with the grin gave me. I never had these shivers before. I couldn't think about it so I walked on. Gal stops a couple of seconds an shouts after me,

Everybody sooked their Maw's diddies so they did... everybody done it.

He was sure this was a fact but I knew he was wrong. His big brothers were probably takin the mince out him again. Sometimes you could take the mince out Gal dead easy. He looked at the **shock horror** on ma face an gave me the look he keeps for when he wins an argument or somethin. I thought of ma

Maw an her diddies but try as I might I couldn't put me on one of them. I couldn't even put Gal on his Maw's. I mean what would you want to do that for? I spat hard on the ground so that he knew I never liked what he was sayin an walked on stampin ma feet an walkin right into trees that never got out the road.

Gal walked even faster with his arms folded an his head tucked in. He never bothered about all the branches that were whackin him on the head. I knew he still felt he won an argument. He looked a lot bigger than he really was so I brought him back to his right size by whackin him right between the soldier blades with a big clump of moss an black gooey stuff that grows up The Lochs. He fell kiddin on he was dead. I walked over to him.

Right. I can member when I was two, I goes. He sits up an looks at me an tries to wipe the muck off his back with the back of his hand.

When you were two? Right yar, he drawled at me forcin out a laugh. I hated when he forced out a laugh. That was worse than just plain havin to laugh. I stood up taller than I'd been all day.

Aye… that's it. When I was two. We lived in Drumpark Street… an ma Da was there… an I was scared… an.

Gal pulls down a rhododendron branch an sits on it lookin at me so that I know he's ready to listen to a story.

Want me to tell you then?

I asks him just to make sure he's not in one of them moods were he kids on he's listenin just so that he can slag you rotten the first mistake you make. He looks at me an I know that he wants to listen to a story.

Aye… all right then… go on… I'll soon tell if you're tellin lies.

He nods his head so that I know he's goin to be quiet an

listen. He plucks a long grass an sticks it between his teeth for suckin while he's listenin. I pluck one too but I hold it in ma hand like a kind of pointer that Teachers use. I pulls down another bit of the tree. I only pulled down a bit of the tree to sit on cause Gal done it but we always seemed to do the same things me an him so we did. We never missed a chance to be the same if we could help it... that's how it used to worry me that we were different in a lot of ways. Sometimes I used to think that he wanted us to be the one person. I should've asked Gal. I'll probably never know now.

Come on Derruck Danyul Riley get on with the story... I'm waitin.

Right, I says rubbin ma hands to show him that I'm just about to start.

Right well. I member when I was two. I must've been two cos I can't member bein anythin before I was three an nobody could ever member bein one could they! We stayed down in Drumpark Street at the time, mind I telt ye about all that?

Gal nods right quick a lot of times so that I know I've to hurry up with the story.

Aye, well, we were in Kirkwood at the time. It was night time an The House was dead quiet so it was. All the other wanes were sleepin. I can't mind if I got out the bed or fell out it or anythin but I member standin at the bottom of the stairs in the dark lobby. We never had no carpets nor nothin in the lobby so it was like nearly bein outside. The floor was right smooth an hard an cold. A draft was blowin in from the scullery but at the same time I could feel heat squeezin out from the kitchen door onto ma toes with the light but I never heard no noise.

I just stopped tellin you the story like I telt it to Gal cos you might not know that in Coatbridge the scullery was what you call the kitchen an the kitchen was what you call the livin room.

It's like as if the folks in Coatbridge took all their things down a level cos they never felt right about bein equal cos they were right poor an not too clever nor nothin an they couldn't speak the right posh way that some folks like Doctors an Teachers an that spoke.

Aye. There was a cold in the lobby an a warm glow comin out from under the kitchen door. I mind it... standin there with ma elbows squeezin into ma sides an all ma fingers in ma mouth hopin somebody would come an get me. Magine. As if anybody's goin to walk along the lobby in the middle of the night. All I had on was a vest an I started shiverin, except for ma toes. They were roastin now in the light at the bottom of the door. I was too scared to stand there an too scared to go in. Next thing I'm on the other side of the door. Honest to God Gal (I blessed myself at that bit so Gal'd believe me better) it was like magic. I'll swear to the end of ma days that I was magic'd through that door so that I never stood there all night to freeze to death from the windy scullery. So there's ma Da sittin me down in a chair. It was roastin in there. The chair was next to a coal fire an it's roarin away an gettin sucked up the chimney everytime the wind whistles round The House. I sat there lookin at him. I can't member what he was doin but I was curled up with ma knees near ma head an ma hands clamped between ma legs. That's when I noticed that the bottom of the vest was wet. I had peed the bed.

I looks at Gal for a split second to see if he was goin to slag me or laugh at me peein the bed but he just nodded again like he was likin the story. So I goes on.

I was grabbin onto the bottom of the vest an tryin to stretch it over ma legs. Then I'm sittin there with a clean one on. A big tent of white. It must've been one of his. I think he magic'd me into that too cos I don't member getting peed one off. An

another thing, I couldn't smell the pee any more. Like he
magic'd me clean too. I was gettin hotter an hotter now an the
fire's jumpin this way then that way. I stared in it tryin to see
when the flame stopped an the coal started. Next thing this big
orange was magic'd into the room. Man it sploded all over the
kitchen. Then I was chewin a bit with ma whole face cos it was
strong as anythin. Ma Da laughed so I laughed back then he just
magic'd me away somewhere that must be all black cos I don't
member nothin about after that for years an years. But see that
orange? Man I can still taste it. Every time I members that time I
see a big shining orange first, then I can taste it an then the
story that I just telt ye comes into ma bones.

Gal knew I was finished cos I stands up an rubs ma hands
again so we could walk on. I knew he was waitin for me to ask
him the farthest back thing that he could member but I never
asked him. You could tell he was itchin to tell some story but I
never even asked him. I walked on through the trees. Sometimes
I done things like that. It never made me feel good and it never
made me feel bad. I just done it and that was that.

He gave up by jumpin on a branch an swingin himself up
there an droppin back to the ground again. I kept on walkin
over to the bridge that went over The Canal an he followed. All
the birds we liked were flappin an swoopin. Swallows an stuff.
We never went near the farm any more cos the Farm Boy
attacked us one time when we were searchin for eggs. He
stoated the nut right on Gal so Gal screamed an ran about like a
blind chicken tryin to hold the blood in his nose. He came at me
big step after step. It was like he was shakin the ground with his
feet. He was five times the size of us. I should've helped Gal but
all I could do was crush myself into a corner hopin that the Farm
Boy never seen me. He did. He came at me an spring-loaded his
head to belt one on me. I don't know what it was. I looked right

brave but I was terryfied so I was. But this is what happened. He fires the nut at me but I drops ma head an he ends up stickin the nose on me. That was the first real fight I ever had with anybody that wasn't Gal. You can't really count all them Square Goes with Gal. The Farm Boy staggers back an starts doin the same dance as Gal. Any sensible person would've laughed their heads off at them two bumpin about the yard holdin the blood in, but not me. I was that scared when he attacked me that I lets out this big giant scream. I mind Gal even looked up. I flies at Farm Boy punchin like a madman. Ma Da never showed me that. I just punched an screamed an swore an punched; even when he wasn't screamin any more I kept on hittin him. I mind bein scared in case he got up an battered me for givin him a doin an that's how I kept on punchin him. Gal came over an had a couple of swipes at him. The thing was, he was about fourteen that boy, so he was. Man was I the hero for that one. Boy the Gal knew how to boost me up in a story. *Lifted the Farm Boy right off the ground with one punch,* Gal'd be sayin to everybody. He started greetin for his Mammy so we bolted the course. We sloped along the side of the wall an then ran like the clappers up to The Railway Bridge. I knew Gal'd boost me up but I never asked him about how good I was an who he thought I could beat at fightin now after that performance. I was that good that I could be one of the best fighters for ma age group in the town. I kept tellin Gal how good his swipes must've been so that he'd know that I want him to boost me up too, just in case he forgot. I sticks my chest out an my chin an walks out in front of Gal so as he can see me when he's thinking how to tell the story later on. Anyway we never went by there any more. We said it was in case he got The Polis for us but I was scared in case he got us an done us right in.

Mental Terry

Hey youse ya pair a tubes... get over here now.

Terry McKenzie's stood there stickin his chest out an pointin stiff to the ground. It's like he's stopped right in the middle of a disco dance. I looks at Gal. Gal looks at me. There's no sense runnin away from Terry. I mean we could run away in different directions. We could run away in the same direction an he'd never catch us cos he smoked an drank. He was fourteen an he was **men—tal**. The reason we never ran away from him is he lived beside us an he'd give us a kickin every time he saw us if we never stopped.

Yous better move it or I'll malky the two of ye.

Right Terry, we're comin.

Me an Gal ran over to him. We're that fast the dust from the ash road's blowin up an smokin around us.

Terry McKenzie was kickin away at the road with the heel of his boot. When you looked when you were runnin towards him all you could see was the puffs of black smoke mixed with the smoke from his fag an the sparks from the steel seggs he hammered into the heel of his boot. You could see the dark outline of his body an his teethy yellow grin below his piggy eyes. It was like the rest of the world had disappeared. He scared me that guy. We get next to him. I'm too scared to say anythin but Gal had big brothers that could do McKenzie no problem so he speaks.

How... how... how'ye doin Terry ma man?

I could tell that Gal was tryin to act tough but you could see he was terryfied.

Shut yer gub.

He grabs Gal by the jumper an lifts him clean off the ground.

Get yer pockets emptied.

Haint got nothin!

Gal was nearly greetin. I wished I could melt a few into McKenzie's face but I was too scared. Gal pulled his pockets out an McKenzie inspected them.

Socks!

We looks at him.

Get the socks off ya perra toerags.

Ma Da...

ZZZININININININING

A big blue flash. I guessed he must've scudded me a good hard punch. I was on the ground.

You shut yer mouth. If any the two of youse tells anybody I'll cut out yer tongues.

SHZZKHLICK

He flicks open a flick-knife.

That's a goo... goo... good knife Terry.

Gal stood there pullin his last sock off an smilin the way a dog does if its been kicked round The House by its owner. McKenzie stuck the knife up at Gal's neck an laughed.

Get yer socks on they're mingin. An tell that boufin oul Maw of yours to get them washed. An don't hang them out on a Friday cos that's when ma burd comes down to see me.

Right yar Terry... I'll tell her... I'll make sure she hangs them out on a Monday Terry... is that OK... Monday?

I was listenin to Gal an I felt angry at him an McKenzie but I felt sorry for Gal as he struggled to get his socks back on. I really wanted to do McKenzie in.

ZZZZZININININININING

I was pickin myself off the ground an he booted me one in the head. Down I goes like a bag a spuds. He jumps on ma back an pulls ma head back by the hair. He sticks the knife on ma neck.

So ye think yer a wee hardman eh?

No... no...

Whit d'ye say I stick this chib right in yer neck?

Please... I'll... no...

I could hear his laugh echo round the countryside an bounce off everywhere an come back at me. Next thing you know Gal's lookin at me an screamin. McKenzie lets go an I flops to the ground.

Shut yer mouth Gallacher.

I see Gal strugglin with McKenzie as I get up out of the cloud of dust. They're starin at ma neck. That's when I felt like a Danny Long Legs had landed on me. I slaps it to kill it an when I take ma hand away its covered in blood. So I thinks *what a lot of blood just for a Danny Long Legs* an then I screams all at the same time cos it all fits thegether now.

He's stabbed me... I'm goin to die... my God!

Sh Sh Sh Sh Sh Sh Sh Sh Sh Sh!

McKenzie's tryin to shut me up an now he's jumpin about like a chicken.

Here... here... I'll give you this... an this... an this.

I peel out the side of ma eye but still wander about like I'm dyin. I mind to keep ma hand on the wound cos its stopped bleedin an I don't want them to know. McKenzie's handin all sorts of money an fags an a knife to Gal to get him to get me not to tell anybody that he stabbed me.

Let me see that cut in your neck.

He says that all concerned like he's ma Maw now an I can feel his smoky breath on ma face. By this time Gal's got all the goodies stuffed up his jumper an he's flickin the knife in an out. McKenzie knows it's only a scratch now but at the same time when he's about to belt me another he thinks of ma Da. You can see that he's thought *Oh Christ his Da is krazy... he'll kill me if he sees the blood and knows about the knife* so he gets all nicey nicey again.

Tell you what... If you promise... cross your heart hope to die... swear on yer Maw's life... not to tell nobody... just say it was a tree or somethin... well... I'll let ye keep all the stuff that I gave youse an I'll tell you where there's a nest... a Stukkie's. With five Yunks in it.

You should've seen me an Gal. The scratch on ma neck healed up right away an our eyes lit up like car lights.

Where is it? Where is...

Promise?

I'll not tell nobody Terry... I'll say that I fell out a tree an there was a bottle on the ground an I just avoided it an it cut me a wee bit.

Right... right...

Gal interrupted him just so that he knew.

An ye can't take the stuff back off us when ye see us again... an ye can't do us in ever again in our lifes!

Aye... right... that an all... the nest's up there in the wall at the left-hand side as ye go under The Railway. It's right above the T where I sprayed TERRY YA BASS an CADZOW BOOT BOYS RULE RA MOON.

By this time Gal is dashin away. He's makin it look like he's only dashin cos of the nest but I know he's dashin to get away from McKenzie an all. McKenzie walks away right quick so I follows Gal. I had a look round at McKenzie an he sparked the heels of his boots an sent clouds of smoke up in the air. I thought I heard him laughin but it might've been just the last bits of his other laugh comin back from its echo on a place far away. I caught up with Gal.

He was a right mean bastard that Terry McKenzie so he was. You could see that some people were wild an that but this guy was mental. A right crackpot. Gal had six bob an some coppers. **We were rich!** An he had a navy lighter an a wee tin of that petrol that you put in it an a packet of flints. He flicked the knife in an out in an out in an out an tried to keep its flicks in time with our steps. We never said a thing about what happened back there cos we couldn't boost each other up much about that. We probably could've done him in, the two of us but he'd get us when we went back down the road. We were beat there all right. Gal was flickin the knife faster an faster an walkin faster an faster.

Shut that thing up Gal.

I didn't shout. It was annoyin me but I just said it like I was talkin to somebody in a tent. He stopped but you could tell he wasn't bothered. You could see the wall were the nest was from where we were.

Well Derruck... there's the nest. D'ye think he's tellin lies? He always lies... but this time... there might be Yunks in the nest right enough... I mean he's terryfied that you'll tell yer Da about the knife an all that.

You could see the names an the stuff he sprayed on the wall makin themselves appear on the wall as we got closer an closer. First you could see:

T RY YA BAS
C ZOW BO T BOYS
rU E RA M N

I had ma eyes jammed right above the T where he said the

nest was. The rest of the letters were paintin themselves onto the wall cos we were gettin right close. I was lookin about so nobody would see us gettin into the nest. The T was high up so I'd've to give Gal a heave-up to get some of the Yunks out to look at. I always wanted to keep them but Gal made me put them back every time we found a nest with Yunks in it. Nobody was about. We got right next to the wall.

TERRY YA BASS
CADZOW BOOT BOYS
RULE RA MOON

It was big white letters sprayed like balloons. He was good a sprayin on walls an they all used to say that he was the best Vandal in our bit. Me an Gal never liked Vandalisin places. We could've been great Vandals so we could but we never bothered. We liked explorin an stuff like I'm tellin you about the now.

The only thing was, above the T where he said there was a nest, it never looked like there was a nest there. I mean a lot of the times you could never tell a place where there was a nest. Gal was good at that but even he was only right three times out of ten. But it was easy to tell where there was no nest an this place right there above the T looked like a place where there was no nest.

There's no nest up there, says Gal.

I was just about to tell him that's what I thought when somethin grabbed ma eye back to where there was no nest. All the wall was brown sandstone that they use on railway bridges an that but there above the T it was black. We got right up next to it. Gal looks up. He had his hands on his hips in a thinkin position. I could tell that he thought somethin but he never told me what he was thinkin.

Give us a heave up there.

I clasped ma fingers thegether an hung them down so he could get a foot in them. He wrapped his arms round ma neck an heaved up. I hated this bit. He puts his foot on ma soldier an clambers up the wall surface. Then he puts his other foot on ma other soldier. Man it digs right in you can't take it but you've got to. I hears him footerin about up there a lot longer than normal even if there was a nest. I hear rustlin like there is a nest there.

EEEEEUCH!

Next thing I know he's flyin by ma head an he lands with a thump so that his footprints echo all round the bridge. It was like a tunnel that bridge that's why everythin echoed in it so much as that. I stared as he stood up. I had got two frights:

1. When he screamed.
2. When he jumped an landed on the ground.

He was holdin somethin in his hands an leanin over lookin at it. I moved closer.

The bastard… the cruel bastard… McKenzie.

Gal started to greet. I could smell petrol. I leaned over to see what he was lookin at. His greetin was rollin round the tunnel like thunder. He's holdin this thing out. His hands are all black an there's a funny smell like when the dinner gets burnt.

That bastard McKenzie… look what he done!

I looks into the thing. I bolts the course when it gets to ma brain what it really is. I runs round in circles shoutin,

OH MAN OH MAN OH MAN OH MAN... OH MAN OH MAN OH MAN OH MAN... OH MAN OH MAN OH MAN OH MAN... OH MAN OH MAN OH MAN OH MAN... OH MAN OH MAN OH MAN OH MAN...

I can't stop. I'm takin big deep breaths an turnin all shades. Next thing up it comes... BOAK all over the place. Gal's sick too. He pulls the hangin slabbers off his lips an walks away an gets this box that's lyin on the grass. He puts the nest in it.

That bastard had poured petrol on the Yunks an lit them. I looked up an two Stukkies were sittin on the fence lookin at us. They never flapped round or shouted an bawled like the Blackies they just sat there. They probably couldn't move or mibbi they sat there an starved themselves to death I don't know but I kept thinkin that they must think that me an Gal were the same an we go around mudderin Chicks an that. We had one last look at the nest. They were like little lumps of burnt wood only you could see white bones an red an pink bits stickin through an you could smell they weren't wood. We took the box away an dug a hole with a paylin off a fence an buried them. I never told Gal but I said an Our Father an three Hail Marys as we were walkin away from the grave.

Strangler Joe

We donnered across the fields where they played rugby an stuff
like that, stuff that we never played. Man this was a weird place,
just over at The Golfie they played at cricket... **CRICKET!**

*C'mon we'll head through that jungley bit there an it'll bring
us out at The Lochs Derruck.*

The jungley bit he was talkin about was all these rhododendron trees planted so as you couldn't see the big tip where they
dumped all the rubbish. There were about five million seagulls
sat in that tip. You should've seen them. Man it was like snow
that was alive. If you lobbed a brick right into them they'd all
jump up an flap their wings nearly at the same time. There were
so many seagulls that their wings used to hit thegether when
they all took off at the same time an some of them would slap
other ones back down into the rubbish. We were fed up annoyin
the seagulls. It was good at first but you grow out of that kind
of stuff an end up explorin an that.

Anyway we walked over to the trees. There was a path that
was made by all the people that must've walked up this way for
years an years. *That's a bit of luck*'s what I said to myself when I
seen him that was on The Pipe an looked like he was followin us
over The Golfie. He was walkin through the tip an the seagulls
were risin in front of him an fallin again behind him as he
walked. I mind thinkin that it just looked like he was a big movin
hole in snow. You could see the blackness of him an you could
make out his hat an that.

Then the bones in ma back shivered... he was holdin a boy by
the scruff of the neck. You could see the boy in red an I knew it
was a boy cos of the way he walked. He never looked like he
was tryin to get away or anythin. They just looked like it was a
boy an his Da was takin him home for doin somethin bad. But it

never felt right so I asked Gal about it.

Gal... mind that guy that we seen in The Golfie... the guy that looked kinda weird?

Aye... what about him?

Gal stopped a lot sharper than you'd've thought he'd stop if you just asked a question about some ordinary guy. You could tell he was scared. He stared at me waitin for me to tell him. I just nodded an pointed ma head at the same time over to the dump where the hole in snow was movin him an the boy across the tip like they were on a magic carpet.

God... that's him all right... an... an he's got a guy with him...
Christ that's Duffy so it is... it's Duffy.

He paused an screwed his eyes up. He always done that when he was tryin to see somethin a lot better did the Gal. You could see he was worried.

What if he's... thingway... what d'ye call him... that Strangler Joe guy that they're an about on the telly an that?

I nods quick at him to see what he was goin to say.

That means that Duffy might get... might get muddered...

D'ye think we should get The Polis...
SHIT! LOOK!

There's the Duffy runnin like a rabbit this way an that way an up an down the hills of ash an rubbish. The Guy's chasin him an cos we're so far away a lot of the times like when Duffy hits the bottom of a slope, we think the mudderer has got him but then he shoots off again in another direction. Man the only thing that's missin is music. It's like a cartoon that's meant to scare you half to death. Gal's fingers are diggin right into ma arm an his teeth are the same tightness as mine an his lips are pulled right back over his teeth an his eyes are wide as golf balls. Duffy jumps off one ash hill onto another one. Bits of dump are smokin an black soot's puffin up into The Sky. They're lost for a minute then Duffy comes **whooshin** through the smoke followed by the arms of the creepy fella. They're runnin round in circles but all the time the wee man's doin well. He's gettin closer an closer to the main Townhead road.

C'mon... C'mon... C'mon... Duffy for Christ sake run... run.

Gal's fingers dig in a bit more every time he says this like he's his Da watchin a horse race. Duffy spins unexpected an

WHAK!

lobs a brick right in the guys face.

On ye go Duffy!

The brick looked like it hit the guy hard cos he stumbled an fell to his knees an shoved his hands into his face. If you looked at him he looked like he was prayin. That's why Gal was cheerin him on like he was boxer now. Duffy bounced off in a straight line towards the road an the guy got to his feet an looked like he was floatin over the ash. Some bits of the dump were on fire now an all. The seagulls were hoverin in the air an screamin so that Duffy an the man looked like they were in one of them silent movies. Just like that the man stoops. I looks an Duffy boy's got hold of a man's arm at the side of the main road.

Right then, a split second before the man on the main road turns to look into the dump, the guy in black varnishes. He just flumps into the ashes an no one can see him. He must've been lyin there. Duffy went along the road with the other guy. We jumped up an down an shouted as loud as we could but the seagulls were cryin too hard an they never heard us they just kept on walkin away. We got on our hunkers an watched the spot where the guy varnished into the ashes. Sure enough he rose up out of there an started to make off in the other way. He kept lookin back all the time when he was walkin away. It was horrible, like his head was on backwards. I was sure he could see us even crouched down in the grass but Gal slapped ma head an said I was daft. But it wasn't ma eyes that thought he had seen us it was somethin else, somethin weird. This was the funniest kind of scared I'd ever been. He varnished into the smoke an Gal started off into the trees.

I'm not goin in there!

I stood with ma arms folded shakin ma head from side to side only with it tilted to the one side a bit to show him that I thought it was daft for anybody to go in there.

But he's away the other way... how could he?

I don't care... I'm just not goin in there... it's too dodgy...

Gal was thinkin a quick plan to get me in there. I could tell he was thinkin a quick plan for that cos he was still leanin into the trees an his legs looked like they were walkin in there anyway. He kept clickin his tongue as he thought. I folded the oul arms a bit tighter so he'd know that only a really good plan would get me in there.

Right then.

I never moved even a wee bit. I just stood there.

If he's lookin for us... an I don't think he is cos he's away in the other bit of The Lochs by now... He's probably from Easterhouse an he's away back there now... But you think he's lookin for us... So if he is... an member he's not... but if he is... is it not easier for him to see us out there in the open? Are we not better in these trees. Jesus we're the best at hidin in trees. An... if anythin does happen... we'll do the Different Ways plan an I'll meet you down at The Loch.

D'ye think he's really from Easterhouse?

AYE.

An ye think he's away home now?

AYE.

An ye think we'll be OK... he'll not come lookin for us nor nothin like that.

AYE! ... I mean no... I mean he's away... we'll be OK... there's no problem... no problem at all.

I kinda believed him so I unfolded the arms an followed him into the trees. I never followed him cause of all that stuff he said cos I still thought that it was Strangler Joe an I still thought that he was out to get me an Gal. The reason I followed him into the trees was cos I was too scared to go the other way on ma own so I had to go with Gal. So that was that. We headed off into the blackness of the inside of the forest an all you could see was chinks of light landin on the ground an shakin about on the grass like as if they were made out of water. The seagulls were quiet now. All that made you know that the dump was there was the stink of the rotten rubbish an the nippy smell of smoke.

It was the terryfiediest I've ever been. Honest to Christ. Think about it. Magine it was you. I kept on tryin not to think about it. You could see that Gal was tryin to not think about it an all. We were walkin along this wee ash path an I was keepin right in the middle. I noticed that Gal kept on turnin round dead slow an lookin with the biggest eyes I've seen on him. We're crunchin along the path an bein glad when we come to this soft quiet bit. It was like we were connected thegether cos we kept stoppin breathin at the exact same time. All the birds were whistlin louder than you ever heard them. You felt like you were in a jungle but it wasn't like when you played at Japs an Marines an that. No way man. This was the real thing. I never knew so many noises before. I've never heard them since. Ma heart's right up there under ma tongue. Gal tries to spit but he can't. He looks kinda white round the face an he's still spinnin round right slow like he's guardin somethin. I'm spinnin too. We're too scared to talk about bein scared so I don't ask him nothin.

Right along the side of the path there's a ditch that's full of murky water. I don't know why but Gal crouches down an starts lookin for frogs an newts. He's leanin between his knees an pokin around in that green stuff so as to make a hole in the water. That's the bit I really member. I stopped turnin an the drops of water plipped into the ditch. A Blackie screamed an some wood pigeons cracked out into The Sky. I breathed right quick an deep an stopped when that breath was half out. I left ma lips wide apart so as no noise would come out. Gal was like a paintin. He went like one of them bits in a film where everythin goes into a dream. I told you that was the bit I membered. It was cos of the things that I thought about. I thought about death. Gal looked like he was just a memory even if the water's ploppin back into the ditch from his hands – he's dead. I cried, not out loud but I cried.

He's sittin there but ma mind's away at his funeral. The whole school's there an they're cryin. Some of the Lassies are screamin an his Maw an Da an all his brothers an sisters are holdin each other up.

I could feel tears runnin down like as if two flies were crawlin down ma face. Gal never looked at me. He just sat there on his hunkers an never turned round. I was lookin at him. I'll tell you this but I don't want you to think there's anythin funny about me but its true.

I'm standin there an I'm terryfied an it's quiet, a scary quiet an Gal's on his hunkers an even the drops of water 've stopped echoin round the place. I'm cryin. I'm sad as anythin an I can't tell why. All I wants to do is go over an throw ma arms around the bold Gal an cuddle him like he's a baby. I never even felt like that when Jesus sent for ma Granda. I never felt like that again in ma whole life up to now.

I'm startin to move ma leg so as to walk over an I swear I was goin to go right over there an cuddle him when all of a suddenly he turns round.

Derruck he says. But he says it right funny like an I stop dead in ma tracks. He stares right into ma eyes for ages an ages. A white bird flies right between our eyes an unclicks them. I can see the trees an the bird in his eyes. They're like mirrors an that's when I see he's been cryin too. Man we were really in contact there… like twins or somethin. I nods the head an so does he. An we knew. We never needed to say nothin so I starts to walk over to him an he starts to walk over to me.

I thought the rattlin leaves on the trees was the white bird that flew through us so I was still walkin over to Gal when the bushes

BURST OPEN.

This leg comes telescopin out the black an dark green. Gal stops like cardboard. His eyes get right wide. The boot of the leg clumps into the soft peat. The body appears an the other leg is leavin the bush. That grin that I told you about, way back on The Pipe that time, appears exactly where the white bird flew into the trees. It was like the white bird flapped into the bush an became that grin an came loupin back out on His face. His eyes swivelled at me but his arm was workin on its own. It came right out the bushes an grabbed Gal by the neck. Gal wriggled like the way a frog does it when you try to hold it. I'm cardboard now an the other arm's comin at me. I can just see this hand an Gal looks like he's screamin but I can't hear him. It's all goin dead an I'm still seein the white bird flyin into the trees. Ma head wants to run but it can't cos of Gal. It's him all right. That guy, on The Pipe an in The Golfie an with Duffy. I can see the slash that the brick made on his face.

Sometimes ma body works before I tell it anythin. Next thing the hand hits me on the soldier cos unknowns to me I've dodged sideways. Strangler Joe tries to make himself stretch so as he can hold onto Gal, who's stopped squirmin now. That's when I take two steps back the way. He's still grinnin like he's happy at somethin an Gal's a rag doll.

C'mere.

Strangler Joe flashes his teeth at me an he's tryin to scare me into goin over to him. I stands stock still an he comes nearer me draggin Gal behind him.

I said C'mere.

What for?
Man was I a cheeky guy there. I don't know where the words got out from but there they were makin their way through the air to Strangler Joe.

Jist got yoursel over here... NOW... Get into these bushes till I search you pair.

I looks at Gal an he's slabberin down his chin an makin this noise like he's chokin. I mind thinkin that Gal's goin to die if I ran away so I thought about goin over to The Strangler. I knew that he never wanted just to search us in the bushes. Man we were already way in the darkest part of the forest anyhow.

Get over here now ya wee runt or, so help me God, I'll choke the livin daylights outa him.

He gives Gal an extra choke at that bit an he lets out a squeak. A feelin went right into me like an electric shock or like as if the wind was blowin right through ma middle. It made me cold an that was when I was sure that me an Gal were goin to be dead. I member decidin to stop walkin backwards so as he could get me.

Well! My God, wait to you hear this. I stops an the grin gets wider an disappears round the side of his face. The blood on his skin cracks and you can see hundreds of white lines like lightnin. I looks at Gal so as he'll know that I'm not runnin away an leavin him. Does the bold Gal not do the maddest thing? Does he not give me one of them looks he saves for when he's just catched a frog an it's in his hand an he's goin to show me it all shinin an slippy. The Joe fellah's nearly at me an his hand's reachin out so as to grab onto ma neck. I hear me swallowin in ma ears an I peed myself just a bit. Somethin clicked an I thought that The Strangler had just clacked his teeth thegether like it was somethin he done before he kilt ye.

It was right dark in them trees but Gal's eyes shone like two bubble floats an I was all mixed up. He looked kind of happy. This is the way it happened. Joe's hand grabs ma throat. It's like a rope goin round it an I'm thinkin that it's so tight there's no way I'm goin to wriggle loose. I've just got this thought in ma head when I sees a shining in the trees. Joe starts to spin me round so as me an Gal are thegether. We bump arms an I sees the shiny thing curvin through the air like a jet rocket. Joe lets out this scream an lets us go. We fall in the same bundle an Joe's holdin his leg on the ground. Gal bounces to his feet.

Run Derruck he's a mudderer… he's a mudderer.

Joe slides into the murky ditch an the black water splashes

up. I sees blood. Gal shoves me.

Different ways... different ways...

Gal bolts the course an so do I. We're runnin different ways an as I take off slippin in the mud Joe gets a grabber out at me an I sees the knife stickin out his leg. But I'm Billy Whizz. The fastest runner in Cadzow. I gets a few trees between me an that ditch before I looks back an can't see him. I thought, *he must've made after Gal*, but I kept on goin. I got faster an I got scareder so I got faster an got scareder. The branches were whippin off ma face an sometimes I fell an got back up before I knew I fell. I whacked the shin off this other branch but I never felt a thing cos I was goin so fast. It was all

trees

trees

trees

an blackness so dark that I thought, I'm never goin to get away, then

THE SKY

THE LOCHS

The Lochs

I ran over to two fishers standin at the edge but I never told them nothin. I just stood there so as the mudderer couldn't get me if he came out the trees. I keeps scannin the trees with ma eyes an ma ears for the bold Gal.

I'm standin there an I'm even more scared now than when we were dead for sure. Ages go by an all there is is the lappin of the water on the shore an the murmurs of the fishers an dogs barkin in the distance. I can't hear a thing from the trees an them flies start to crawl down ma cheeks again.

I mind spinnin away so the fishers couldn't see me cryin an I bit into ma bottom lip. The clouds rollin over the trees were gettin faster an faster an every now an then I thought I heard the crack of a twig. Ma heart started to get faster but then it got slowed right down again by the quietness.

That's when I started to pray. I really thought The Strangler had got Gal an choked him to death. I said the prayers into myself but I had to put ma hands up at ma face cos sometimes ma lips moved an sometimes they never.

Hail Mary...

I looks round so that nobody's watchin me.

... fulla grace...

I look into the trees... nothin! I felt like givin in... in fact for a wee minute I thought what if there was no Hail Mary an no God but I prayed on.

... the Lord is with thee...

I stops an listens dead quiet. A couple of dogs bark again an the water gurgles under an oul log. I thinks about me an the world an all the stars an no God nor nothin but I figured I was just terryfied an prayed on.

Blessed art thou among women...

The clouds got faster an the tree tops started to bend in the wind. It was like they were pointin at me.

an blessed is the fruit...

It's mad but I thought of Gal laughin an his white teeth shining in the sun an him scrunchin into an apple we got from the trees at the back of The Wine Alley. I never bothered tryin to hide the tears now.

... of thy woom Jesus...

I kidded on I was lookin for somethin on the ground so that I could bow the head a bit. You've got to bow the head at that bit the Teacher says.

Holy Mary...

I looked up at The Sky half expectin to see Hail Mary glowin away there an smilin like it was all goin to be all right but all I could see was the clouds gettin darker and faster.

... Mother a God prayfrus sinners...

Still nothin from the trees.

Now an at the hour of our death.

I looks up at The Sky again. This time I wondered who the hell I'm talkin too. Nothin changed. Still no Gal. I listened. The wind was gettin up an far away you could hear the chickens crowin in the farmyard.

AMEN!

I shouts. I shouts it like a swear word. The dogs stop barkin an the fishers look round. The water shoved itself onto ma feet but I never moved I just stood on it. A railway sleeper touched a rock an floated off into the distance. A crack appeared in the clouds an a blitz of light showered the rock. The clouds closed. The chickens croaked an the dogs ran away to the woods.

I went to go to the fishers to tell them about Gal when there he was. Man I was so happy... I can see him now... he's runnin through the trees. He's not lookin forward an he's not lookin back, he's just rattlin through them leaves an branches like a boy in a film. Then you could see that he knew he was comin to the end of the woods cos he sprinted even harder an then jumped right out onto the path.

He sees me.

I sees him.

You'd've thought we'd run at each other like them eejits on the beach at the end of Love Films but we never. We walked towards each other like the way we always do. We never screamed or shouted. It's the first time I member walkin like a man over the path.

Close one there Gal?

Gal was still tryin to get his breath back so we walks away from The Lochs in silence. I listened to his breathin so I could start to tell him how brave we were an all that stuff.

You showed him there all right Gal.

Aye.

He looked away at the trees an I thought that he must be keepin a look out for The Strangler.

You lookin for The Strangler so as you can get him again Gal? Is that what your game is? Aye, Gal, man you could've done him right in... ye could've stuck that knife right through his heart... or... or his neck.

I stops so that he can take over an tell me about the instant he stuck the blade in but he never said nothin. I goes on a bit more.

Ma Da says that when you stick a bayonet in somebody it's the same feelin as when you stick a knife through an orange...

Derruck...

What?

Goin to not talk about it I feel sick...

Aye... right enough Gal I nearly boaked after I ran through the trees...

He grabbed ma soldier an span me round. He never needed to tell me cos when I looked in his eyes I knew that it wasn't the runnin that made him sick.

It's not the runnin... it's...

He was rubbin his hand madly off his trouser leg. There was blood on his fingers. He dived into the trees an grabbed a bunch of leaves an started to rub them the way you rub soap. Next thing he plunged his hands into the ditch water. He looks at me. He looked angry an scared at the same time.

Don't tell nobody about it... right.

Right Gal... I won't say nothin to nobody about nothin... honest to God cross ma heart hope to die.

Ma eyes couldn't stop themselves swivellin to the bruise on his neck. It was like somebody squashed a plumb into his skin. He pulled his jumper up onto it.

Just say that I fell out a tree an skelped ma neck off a branch on the way down.

Were you knocked out?

No... just stunned a bit... an blind for a couple of seconds.

Did I go an get anybody... The Polis or somethin?

No... I was all right an we played the rest of the day...

He thinks an presses his fingers on his top lip.

... we played the rest of the day an we never seen the bruise till we looked in a shop window...

But how did I not see it then?

Oh aye... well... we found some oul bits of cloth an tied them round our necks so we could kid on we were gypsies.

We went on like that all the way home. By the time we got there we had a magic story to tell. I don't know what he telt his Maw an Da but I know one thing, he never mentioned the knife or Strangler Joe ever again. Well, that's ma story like it or lump it an the only thing is you'd better watch who you tell cos I promised Gal not to tell nobody about it.

I always thought about it... They never caught Strangler Joe so you might know him. He's got a brick mark on his face and a big stab wound in his right leg; that's how you'll know him if you ever suspect someone of bein him.

There was another fright that we got that day. When we turned the corner into the lane the place was buzzin with Fuzz. You could see the black uniforms an the shining buttons an the white cars with the blue lights at the bottom of the lane. Gal looks at me an I looks at him. I was sure that we were goin to get done with tryin to kill The Strangler. The colour drained out the two of us.

Mick Rettie comes runnin up. Me an Gal snuck back behind the fence at the top so as nobody could see us.

Mick... Mick...

Gal used his shout-whisper. He was great at that.

Mick turned as he was goin in his gate an saw us through the fence.

Awright Gal. Awright Derruck.

His eyes lit up. We never needed to ask him. The story came fallin out.

The Polis came down an lifted Duffy an all them that run about with him. I think they derailed a train. All the Maws an Das have been out fightin in the lane sayin it was everybody else's son that done it... but they don't know what it's about yet... man it's been great so it has... yous've missed yoursels where have you been anyway?

I looks at Gal. He looks at me. The two of us laugh.

Egg collectin.

I said that an looked at Gal so as he could carry on with the lie. I was good at short lies but Gal was good at big long ones.

Get anythin good?

Mick's eyes lit up in case we had anythin to show him.

Nah nothin not a thing.

He was disappointed an walked away in his gate. Me an Gal shoved our hands in our pockets an shuffled down the lane. Nobody even noticed us cause of all what was goin on. We marched down the lane in step.

Click.

His gate.

Click.

Ma gate.

Seven o'clock.

Seven o'clock.

Slam. His door.

Slam. Ma door.

Hiya Da

Hiyi son.

He looks.

What's that mark on your neck?

I touches ma neck lightly.

We were up The Lochs... an... an we were on this tree... an... an...

The door closes an I can hear the music for the News.

The door opens an ma Maw comes out.

That Duffy was jist on the telly there... nearly got himsel kilt with Strangler Joe the day... up at the Council Tip she goes... so that's what all The Polis were about. She stares at me.

Now you mind an stay away from that Railway... an that Pipe... an up them Lochs... d'ye hear me?

She walked away before I could tell her I could hear her loud and clear. All I could see was her bum.

Some other books published by **Luath** Press

Six Black Candles
Des Dillon
ISBN 1 84282 053 2 PB
£6.99

Picking Brambles and Other Poems
Des Dillon
ISBN 1 84282 021 4 PB
£6.99

'*Where's Stacie Gracie's head?*'
... sharing space with the sweetcorn and two-for-one lemon meringue pies ... in the freezer.

Caroline's husband abandons her (bad move) for Stacie Gracie, his assistant at the meat counter, and incurs more wrath than he anticipated. Caroline, her five sisters, mother and granny, all with a penchant for witchery, invoke the lethal spell of the Six Black Candles. A natural reaction to the break up of a marriage?

The spell does kill. You only have to look at the evidence. Mess with these sisters, or Maw or Oul Mary and they might do the Six Black Candles on you. But will Caroline's home ever be at peace for long enough to do the spell and will Caroline really let them do it?

Set in present day Irish Catholic Coatbridge, *Six Black Candles* is bound together by the power of traditional storytelling and the strength of female familial relationships. Bubbling under the cauldron of superstition, witchcraft and religion is the heat of revenge; and the love and venom of sisterhood.

Hilarious THE MIRROR

An exciting, entertaining read... just buy it. THE BIG ISSUE

I always considered myself to be first and foremost a poet. Unfortunately nobody else did. The further away from poetry I moved the more successful I became as a writer. This collection for me is the pinnacle of my writing career. Simply because it is my belief that poetry is at the cutting edge of language. Out there breaking new ground in the creation of meaning.
DES DILLON

A superb collection which easily matched his award winning novels for quality.
JIM CRAIG

Both sensual and spiritual, this is a seductive collection.
JANET PAISLEY

This is a collection which beats with a full, tough heart, and thrums like good music. ALAN BISSETT

Through his poetic soul a big, big heart and a soft underbelly.
LESLEY BENZIE

A refreshing, individual style. His words are like brambles – big and succulent, whether fruity or beefy. There is a certain downbeat mood too, a weight, like the words have a fist inside them... Dillon is surely set to become one of our most powerful poetic voices.
SCOTTISH BOOK COLLECTOR

FICTION

Outlandish Affairs: An Anthology of Amorous Encounters
Edited and introduced by Evan Rosenthal and Amanda Robinson
ISBN 1 84282 055 9 PB £9.99

Driftnet
Lin Anderson
ISBN 1 84282 034 6 PB £9.99

The Fundamentals of New Caledonia
David Nicol
ISBN 0 946487 93 6 HB £16.99

Milk Treading
Nick Smith
ISBN 1 84282 037 0 PB £6.99

Road Dance
John MacKay
ISBN 1 84282 024 9 PB £9.99

But n Ben A-Go-Go
Matthew Fitt
ISBN 0 946487 82 0 HB £10.99
ISBN 1 84282 014 1 PB £6.99

The Strage Case of RL Stevenson
Richard Woodhead
ISBN 0 946487 86 3 HB £16.99

POETRY
Tartan and Turban
Bashabi Fraser
ISBN1 84282 044 3 PB £8.99

Drink the Green Fairy
Brian Whittingham
ISBN 1 84282 020 6 PB £8.99

The Ruba'iyat of Omar Khayyam, in Scots
Rab Wilson
ISBN 1 84282 046 X PB £8.99

Kate o Shanter's Tale and other poems
Matthew Fitt
ISBN 1 84282 028 1 PB £6.99 (book)
ISBN 1 84282 043 5 £9.99 (audio CD)

Talking with Tongues
Brian Finch
ISBN 1 84282 006 0 PB £8.99

Immortal Memories
John Cairney
ISBN 1 84282 009 5 HB £20.00

Madame Fifi's Farewell
Gerry Cambridge
ISBN 1 84282 005 2 PB £8.99

Scots Poems to be Read Aloud
Introduced by Stuart McHardy
ISBN 0 946487 81 2 PB £5.00

Poems to be Read Aloud
Introduction by Tom Atkinson
ISBN 0 946487 006 PB £5.00

Bad Ass Raindrop
Kokumo Rocks
ISBN 1 84292 018 4 PB £6.99

Sex, Death & Football
Alistair Findlay
ISBN 1 84282 022 2 PB £6.99

Men and Beasts: Wild Men and Tame Animals
Valerie Gillies and Rebecca Marr
ISBN 0 946487 928 PB £15.00

The Whisky Muse: Scotch Whisky in Poem and Song
Robin Laing
ISBN 1 84282 041 9 PB £7.99

THE QUEST FOR
The Quest for Robert Louis Stevenson
John Cairney
ISBN 0 946487 87 1 HB £16.99

The Quest for the Nine Maidens
Stuart McHardy
ISBN 0 946487 66 9 HB £16.99

The Quest for the Original Horse Whisperers
Russell Lyon
ISBN 1 84282 020 6 HB £16.99

The Quest for the Celtic Key
Karen Ralls-MacLeod and Ian Robertson
ISBN 1 84282 031 1 PB £8.99

The Quest for Arthur
Stuart McHardy
ISBN 1 84282 012 5 HB £16.99

FOLKLORE
The Supernatural Highlands
Francis Thompson
ISBN 0 946487 31 6 PB £8.99

Tall Tales from an Island
Peter Mcnab
ISBN 0 946487 07 3 PB £8.99

Luath Storyteller: Highland Myths & Legends
George W MacPherson
ISBN 1 84282 003 6 PB £5.00

Scotland: Myth, Legend & Folklore
Stuart McHardy
ISBN 0 946487 69 3 PB £7.99

Tales from the North Coast
Alan Temperley
ISBN 0 946487 18 9 PB £8.99

HISTORY
Scots in Canada
Jenni Calder
ISBN 1 84282 038 9 PB £7.99

Plaids & Bandanas: Highland Drover to Wild West Cowboy
Rob Gibson
ISBN 0 946487 88 X PB £7.99

A Passion for Scotland
David R Ross
ISBN 1 84282 019 2 PB £5.99

Civil Warrior
Robin Bell
ISBN 184282 013 3 HB £10.99

Reportage Scotland: History in the Making
Louise Yeoman
ISBN 0 946487 43 X PB £9.99

SOCIAL HISTORY
Pumpherston: the story of a shale oil village
Sybil Cavanagh
ISBN 1 84282 011 7 HB £17.99
ISBN 1 84282 015 X PB £10.99

Crofting Years
Francis Thompson
ISBN 0 946487 06 5 PB £6.95

Shale Voices
Alistair Findlay
ISBN 0 946487 78 2 HB £17.99
ISBN 0 946487 48 0 PB £10.99

ON THE TRAIL OF
On the Trail of William Wallace
David R Ross
ISBN 0 946487 47 2 PB £7.99

On the Trail of Bonnie Prince Charlie
David R Ross
ISBN 0 946487 68 5 PB £7.99

On the Trail of Robert Burns
John Cairney
ISBN 0 946487 51 0 PB £7.99

BIOGRAPHY
Tobermory Teuchter
Peter Macnab
ISBN 0 946487 41 3 PB £7.99

Bare Feet and Tackety Boots
Archie Cameron
ISBN 0 946487 17 0 PB £7.95

The Last Lighthouse
Sharma Krauskopf
ISBN 0 946487 96 0 PB £7.99

Details of these and other Luath Press titles are to be found at www.luath.co.uk

Luath Press Limited

committed to publishing well written books worth reading

LUATH PRESS takes its name from Robert Burns, whose little collie Luath (*Gael.*, swift or nimble) tripped up Jean Armour at a wedding and gave him the chance to speak to the woman who was to be his wife and the abiding love of his life. Burns called one of *The Twa Dogs* Luath after Cuchullin's hunting dog in *Ossian's Fingal*. Luath Press was established in 1981 in the heart of Burns country, and is now based a few steps up the road from Burns' first lodgings on Edinburgh's Royal Mile. Luath offers you distinctive writing with a hint of unexpected pleasures.

Most bookshops in the UK, the US, Canada, Australia, New Zealand and parts of Europe, either carry our books in stock or can order them for you. To order direct from us, please send a £sterling cheque, postal order, international money order or your credit card details (number, address of cardholder and expiry date) to us at the address below. Please add post and packing as follows: UK – £1.00 per delivery address; overseas surface mail – £2.50 per delivery address; overseas airmail – £3.50 for the first book to each delivery address, plus £1.00 for each additional book by airmail to the same address. If your order is a gift, we will happily enclose your card or message at no extra charge.

Luath Press Limited
543/2 Castlehill
The Royal Mile
Edinburgh EH1 2ND
Scotland
Telephone: 0131 225 4326 (24 hours)
Fax: 0131 225 4324
email: gavin.macdougall@luath. co.uk
Website: www. luath.co.uk